Pinocchio

Illustrated by
FULVIO TESTA

Translated from the Italian by
GEOFFREY BROCK

Introduction by
UMBERTO ECO

ANDERSEN PRESS

Introduction

Carlo Collodi's story of *Pinocchio* first appeared serially between 1881 and 1883, and has since become famous in nearly every language in the world. It must be said first of all that, though written in the nineteenth century, the original *Pinocchio* remains as readable as if it had been written in the twenty-first, so limpid and simple is its prose – and so musical in its simplicity.

However, though it's written in very simple language, *Pinocchio* is not a simple book. I'm tempted to say that it's not even a fairy tale, since it lacks the fairy tale's indifference to everyday reality and doesn't limit itself to one simple, basic moral, but rather deals with many. How else can we explain its universal appeal?

I'm grateful to Geoffrey Brock for bringing it once more (upon a time) to our attention.

Umberto Eco

Chapter 1

Once upon a time there was . . .

"A king!" my little readers will say at once.

No, children, you're wrong. Once upon a time there was a piece of wood.

It wasn't a fancy piece of wood, just a regular woodpile log, the kind you might put in your stove or fireplace to stoke a fire and heat your room.

I don't know how it happened, but the fact is that one fine day this piece of wood turned up in the workshop of an old carpenter, Master Antonio by name, though everyone called him Master Cherry, on account of the tip of his nose, which was always shiny and crimson, like a ripe cherry.

Master Cherry was delighted to see that piece of wood. He rubbed his hands together with satisfaction and mumbled in a soft voice, "This log has turned up at a good moment. I think I'll use it to make me a table leg."

Wasting no time, he picked up his sharp hatchet to start removing the log's bark and trimming it down, but just as he was about to strike the first blow, his arm froze in midair, because he heard a little high-pitched voice pleading, "Don't hit me too hard!"

Just imagine dear old Master Cherry's reaction!

His bewildered eyes roamed the room to see where on earth that little voice had come from, but he didn't see anyone! He looked under his workbench – nobody there. He looked inside a cabinet he always kept shut – nobody there. He looked in his basket of wood shavings and sawdust – nobody there. He even opened his workshop door to take a look in the street – nobody there. So what was going on?

"I see," he said then, laughing and scratching his wig. "Clearly I must have imagined that little voice myself. Now let's get back to work."

And picking the hatchet back up, he dealt the piece of wood a heavy blow.

"Ouch! You hurt me!" cried the same little voice, bitterly.

This time Master Cherry was struck dumb: his eyes bugged out of his head in fright, his mouth gaped, his tongue dangled down to his chin, like those grotesque faces carved on fountains. When he regained the use of speech, he said, trembling and stammering with fear, "That little voice that said *ouch*, where could it have come from? Because

there's not a living soul in this place. Could this piece of wood have somehow learned to cry and complain like a little boy? I can't believe that. Look at this log – it's a piece of firewood, like any other. If I threw it on the fire I could bring a pot of beans to a boil. So what's going on? Could someone be hidden inside it? If anyone's hiding in there, tough luck for him. I'll show him what's what!"

And as he spoke he grabbed that poor piece of wood with both hands and began whacking it mercilessly against the walls of the room.

Then he listened, to see if he could hear a little voice complaining. He waited two minutes, and no voice; five minutes, and no voice; ten minutes, and no voice!

"I see," he said then, forcing a laugh and ruffling his wig. "Clearly I must have imagined it myself, that little voice that said *ouch*. Now let's get back to work."

And because by this point he was really quite afraid, he began humming to himself to pluck up his courage.

Meanwhile, leaving the hatchet aside, he picked up his plane, intending to scrape that piece of wood and make it smooth, but as he was planing back and forth, he heard the same little voice, which laughed and said, "Stop it! You're tickling my tummy!"

This time poor Master Cherry fell down as if struck by lightning. When he opened his eyes again, he found himself sitting on the floor.

His face seemed misshapen, and even the tip of his nose, which was nearly always crimson, had turned bright blue with fright.

Chapter 2

Just then there was a knock on his door.

"Come on in," said the carpenter, still too weak to stand.

In walked a spry old man. His name was Geppetto, but the neighbourhood kids, when they wanted to make him boil with rage, called him by the nickname Corn Head, since his yellow wig looked like a mound of cornmeal mush.

Geppetto had a terrible temper. Heaven help whoever called him Corn Head! He turned instantly into a wild animal and there was no controlling him.

"Good day, Master Antonio," Geppetto said. "What are you doing down there on the floor?"

"I'm teaching the ants to count."

"Well, good for you!"

"What brings you to my shop, my dear Geppetto?"

"My legs. Actually, Master Antonio, I've come to ask a favour."

"Here I am, at your service," the carpenter replied, rising to his knees.

"This morning an idea popped into my head."

"Let's hear it."

"I thought I'd make myself a nice wooden puppet, I mean a really amazing one, one that can dance and fence, and do flips. Then I'd travel the world with it, earning my crust of bread and cup of wine as I went. What do you think?"

"Good idea, Corn Head!" shouted that same little voice, seemingly out of nowhere.

Hearing himself called Corn Head, dear Geppetto turned as red as a hot pepper, and approaching the carpenter he said furiously, "Why are you insulting me?"

"Who's insulting you?"

"You called me Corn Head!"

"It wasn't me."

"Oh, I suppose you're saying it was me? I say it was you."

"Was not."

"Was too."

"Was not!"

"Was too!"

As tempers flared, words gave way to deeds, and they scratched, bit, and battered each other as they fought.

When the fight was over, Master Antonio found Geppetto's yellow wig in his hands, and Geppetto realized that he had the carpenter's grey wig in his mouth.

"Give me back my wig!" shouted Master Antonio.

"And you give me mine back, and we'll make peace."

Returning each other's wigs, the two old men shook hands and swore to remain good friends for the rest of their lives.

"So, dear Geppetto," said the carpenter, as a peace offering, "what is that favour you wanted to ask?"

"I'd like a little wood to make my puppet with – will you give me some?"

Master Antonio, quite happily, went straight to his workbench to fetch the piece of wood that had given him such a fright. But just as he was about to give it to his friend, the piece of wood gave a violent jerk and, breaking free from his grasp, banged against the withered shins of poor Geppetto.

"Oh! So that's how you present your gifts, is it? You've nearly crippled me!"

"I swear it wasn't me!"

"Then I suppose it was me!"

"It was that piece of wood that hit you."

"I know it was the wood, but you're the one who threw it at my legs!"

"I didn't throw it!"

"Liar!"

"Geppetto, don't insult me, or else I'll call you Corn Head!"

"Donkey!"

"Corn Head!"

"Jackass!"

"Corn Head!"

"Ugly ape!"

"Corn Head!"

On hearing himself called Corn Head for the third time, Geppetto flew into a blind rage and hurled himself upon the carpenter, and they went at each other tooth and nail. When the battle had ended, Master Antonio had two more scratches on his nose, and Geppetto had two fewer buttons on his jacket. Having thus evened the score, they shook hands and swore to remain good friends for the rest of their lives.

And so Geppetto took his nice piece of wood, thanked Master Antonio, and went hobbling home.

Chapter 3

Geppetto lived in a small ground-floor room, lit by a single window. The furnishings could not have been plainer: an old chair, a ramshackle bed, and a table that was falling apart. On the rear wall you could see a fireplace with a glowing fire, but it was a painted fire, and above it was a painted pot, which boiled merrily and gave off steam that really looked like steam.

As soon as he got home, Geppetto gathered his tools and got ready to carve and construct his puppet.

"What name should I give him?" he said to himself. "I think I'll call him Pinocchio. That's a lucky name. I once knew an entire family by that name: the father was Pinocchio, the mother was Pinocchia, and the kids were all Pinocchio Juniors, and they got on just fine. The richest one was a beggar."

Now that he had a name for his puppet, he set to work in earnest, carving the hair, then the forehead, then the eyes.

Imagine his surprise when, as soon as the eyes were finished, he saw that they could move and were staring straight at him.

Geppetto didn't like the way those eyes looked at him, and he said in an angry tone, "Wicked wooden eyes, why are you watching me?"

No answer.

Then after the eyes, he made the nose. But no sooner was the nose finished than it started to grow. And it grew and grew and grew, until in a few minutes it had become a huge, nearly endless nose.

Poor Geppetto kept struggling to trim it back down to size, but the more he trimmed it down, the longer that impertinent nose became.

After the nose, he made the mouth.

Before the mouth was even finished, it began to laugh and mock him.

"Stop laughing!" said Geppetto, annoyed. But it was like talking to a wall.

"I said stop laughing!" he yelled in a threatening tone.

The mouth stopped laughing but stuck its tongue all the way out.

Not wanting to damage his own handiwork, Geppetto pretended not to notice and kept on working.

After the mouth, he carved the chin, the neck, the shoulders, the torso, the arms and the hands.

No sooner had he finished the hands than he felt his wig being snatched from his head. And what do you think he saw when he looked up? He saw his yellow wig in the puppet's hand.

"Pinocchio! Give me back my wig at once!"

But Pinocchio, instead of giving the wig back, set it on his own head. He was half swallowed beneath it.

This insolent, mocking behaviour made Geppetto feel more miserable and wretched than he had ever felt in his life, and turning to Pinocchio he said, "What a scamp of a son! You're not even finished yet and already you're treating your father with disrespect. That's bad, my boy, bad!"

And he wiped a tear from his eye.

The legs and feet were still left.

When Geppetto finished making the feet, one of them kicked him in the nose.

"I deserve it!" he said to himself. "I should have known – now it's too late!"

Then he lifted the puppet from under the arms and set him down on the ground so as to make him walk.

Pinocchio's legs were stiff and he didn't know how to move them, so Geppetto led him by the hand, teaching him to put one foot in front of the other.

When his legs loosened up a bit, Pinocchio began to walk by himself and then to run around the room, until he slipped through the door, jumped into the street, and ran off. And there was poor Geppetto running after him, unable to catch him because that puppet was bounding like a rabbit. The clacking of his wooden feet on the pavement made quite a racket, like twenty pairs of farmer clogs.

"Catch him! Catch him!" yelled Geppetto. But the people who were out in the street, seeing this wooden puppet running like a thoroughbred, stopped and watched him with delight. They laughed and laughed and laughed, not believing their eyes.

Finally, and fortunately, a policeman appeared. Hearing all that clatter, and thinking it was some colt that had slipped from its master's grasp, he bravely planted his feet wide in the middle of the road and resolved to stop him and prevent further mayhem.

When Pinocchio saw the policeman blocking the entire road up ahead of him, he figured he'd surprise him by running straight between his legs, but it didn't work.

Without budging an inch, the policeman snatched him up by the nose (it was a prodigiously long nose, one that seemed specially designed to be easily seized by policemen), and delivered him back into Geppetto's arms. Geppetto's first impulse was to give him a good ear-pulling, to set him straight. But imagine his reaction when, looking for Pinocchio's ears, he wasn't able to find them – and do you know why? Because in his haste to finish carving, he had forgotten to make them.

So he grabbed Pinocchio by the nape of his neck and began to lead him back. Shaking his head menacingly, Geppetto said, "We're going home. And you can be sure we'll settle our accounts when we get there."

Pinocchio understood his drift and threw himself to the ground, refusing to take another step. Meanwhile the busybodies and the idlers began to gather into a crowd around them.

They all had their opinions.

"Poor puppet!" some said. "Who can blame him for not wanting to go home! Just imagine how that mean Geppetto would thrash him!"

And the others added spitefully: "That Geppetto seems like a nice man, but he's a real bully with the boys! If they leave that poor puppet in his hands, he might well bust him to pieces!"

In short, they made such a fuss that the policeman set Pinocchio free and took poor Geppetto straight to jail. At a loss for words to defend himself, Geppetto cried like a little calf, and on his way to jail he stammered as he sobbed: "Wicked child! And to think that I worked so hard to make him a proper puppet! But it's my own fault – I should have known what to expect!"

What happened next is so strange you'll scarcely believe it, but I'll tell you all about it in the coming chapters.

Chapter 4

What happened next, children, is that while poor, innocent Geppetto was being led off to jail, that rascal Pinocchio, freed from the policeman's clutches, went sprinting across the fields to get home as fast as he could. Running crazily, he leapt over tall embankments, thorny hedges, and ditches full of water, much like a little goat or rabbit fleeing from hunters. When he got back home, the front door was ajar. He pushed it open and went inside, and as soon as he had bolted the door behind him, he plopped down onto the floor with a great sigh of satisfaction.

But his satisfaction didn't last long, as he heard someone in the room saying, "Cree, cree, cree!"

"Who's calling me?" said Pinocchio, quite alarmed.

"I am!"

Pinocchio turned and saw a large cricket climbing slowly up the wall.

"Tell me, Cricket, who might you be?"

"I'm the Talking Cricket, and I've lived in this room for more than a hundred years."

"Well it's my room now," said the puppet, "and if you'd like to do me a big favour, leave right now and don't look back."

"I won't leave this place," replied the Cricket, "until I've told you a great truth."

"Tell me and make it quick."

"Woe to any little boy who rebels against his parents and turns his back on his father's house! He will come to no good in this world, and sooner or later he'll be filled with bitter regret."

"Sing on, dear Cricket, if it makes you happy. But the fact is I'm leaving this place tomorrow at the crack of dawn, because if I hang around the same thing that happens to all the other kids will happen to me, too: I'll be sent to school, and I'll be expected to study whether I like it or not, and – just between you and me – I have absolutely no desire to study. I'd much rather run around chasing butterflies and climbing trees and catching baby birds."

"You poor little simpleton! Don't you know that if you do that, you'll grow up to be a real jackass and everyone will make fun of you?"

"Hush, you gloom-and-doom Cricket!" yelled Pinocchio. But the Cricket, who was patient and philosophical, instead of taking offence at this rudeness, continued in the same tone.

"And if going to school doesn't suit you, why don't you at least learn an honest trade, so that you can put food on the table?"

"You want to know why?" replied Pinocchio, who was starting to lose his patience. "Of all the trades in the world, there's only one that really suits me."

"And what trade would that be?"

"That of eating, drinking, sleeping, playing, and wandering wherever I like from sunrise to sunset."

"For your information," said the Talking Cricket with his usual calm, "everyone who plies that trade ends up in either a poorhouse or a prison."

"Watch out, you gloom-and-doom Cricket! If I snap, you'll be sorry!"

"Poor Pinocchio! I really feel sorry for you!"

"Why would you feel sorry for me?"

"Because you're a puppet and, what's worse, you're a blockhead."

At these last words, Pinocchio jumped up in a rage, grabbed a wooden mallet from the workbench, and flung it at the Talking Cricket.

Perhaps he didn't mean to hit him at all, but unfortunately he hit him square on the head. With his last breath the poor Cricket cried *cree-cree-cree* and then died on the spot, stuck to the wall.

Chapter 5

Meanwhile darkness had begun to fall, and Pinocchio, who hadn't had a thing to eat, noticed a faint grumbling in his stomach, which felt exactly like appetite.

But appetite in boys grows quickly, and sure enough, after a few minutes his appetite had turned into hunger, and then suddenly it was a wolflike hunger – a hunger you could have cut with a knife.

Poor Pinocchio ran quickly towards the pot that was boiling on the fire and reached out to remove the lid, to see what was inside – but the pot was painted on the wall.

Just imagine how he felt. His nose, which was already long, grew at least four inches longer.

At this point he began to run around the room and rifle through every drawer, every nook and cranny, searching for a little bread, even stale bread, a crust, a dog's bone, a little mouldy corn mush, a fish skeleton, a cherry pip – in short, anything he could chew on. But he found nothing, a big fat nothing, nothing at all.

And meanwhile poor Pinocchio's hunger kept growing and growing. His only relief was yawning, and he yawned so wide that the corners of his mouth met his ears. And after yawning, he would spit, and it felt as though he were spitting out his stomach.

Losing hope, he wept and said, "The Talking Cricket was right. I was wrong to rebel against my daddy and to run away from home. If my daddy was here, I wouldn't be yawning to death now! Oh, what a terrible sickness hunger is!"

Just then he thought he glimpsed, atop a heap of sweepings, something roundish and white that looked very much like a chicken egg. He was up and on it in a single motion – it really was an egg.

Words cannot describe the puppet's joy; you must imagine it yourself. Almost convinced it was a dream, he turned the egg over and over in his hand, touching it and kissing it. And as he kissed it, he said, "Now how should I cook it? I know, I'll make an omelette! No, better to fry it up in a pan. Or maybe it would be tastier if I poached it? Or what if I boiled it instead? No, the quickest way is to fry it up in a pan – I can't wait any longer!"

Wasting no time, he set a small frying pan on a brazier that was full of live coals. Instead of oil or butter, he put a little water in the pan, and when the water began to steam –

crack! – he broke the eggshell and tried to pour its contents into the pan.

But instead of egg white and egg yolk, out came a very cheerful and refined Chick, who bowed handsomely as he said, "A thousand thanks, Sir Pinocchio, for having saved me the trouble of breaking the shell myself! Farewell, take care, and all my best to your family."

With those words, he stretched out his wings and flew through the open window, disappearing from view.

The poor puppet stood there as if bewitched, eyes wide, mouth agape, half an eggshell in each hand. When the shock wore off, he began to weep and wail and stamp his feet on the ground in despair. Through his tears, he said, "So the Talking Cricket was right! If I hadn't run away, and if my daddy was here, I wouldn't be dying of hunger now! Oh, what a terrible sickness hunger is!"

And because his belly was rumbling more than ever and he had no idea how to quiet it, he decided to go out and pay a quick visit to the nearby village, in the hope of finding some charitable soul who might give him a bit of bread.

Chapter 6

It turned out to be a truly dreadful winter night: thunder roared, lightning seemed to set fire to the sky, and a bitter, blustery wind whistled furiously, kicking up dust clouds and making the trees groan and creak across the countryside.

Pinocchio was terribly afraid of thunder and lightning, but his hunger was greater than his fear. And so he dashed out of the door at top speed, and after a hundred or so leaping strides he reached the village, panting, his tongue hanging out like a hunting dog.

But everything was dark and deserted. The shops were closed; the doors of houses were closed; the windows were closed. There wasn't so much as a dog in the street. It looked like the land of the dead.

At this point, Pinocchio, overcome by despair and hunger, ran to the doorbell of a house and began ringing it loudly, telling himself, "Surely someone will come."

Indeed a little old man in a nightcap did come, and he yelled angrily from his window, "What do you want at this hour?"

"Would you be so kind as to give me a bit of bread?"

"Don't move, I'll be right back," replied the little old man, who assumed Pinocchio was one of those annoying miscreants who get their kicks by ringing the doorbells of decent folk, just to prevent them from getting a good night's sleep.

After half a minute the window opened again, and the same little old man shouted, "Stand below me and hold out your hat."

Pinocchio took off his raggedy hat, but when he held it out, a basinful of water drenched him from head to toe, as if he had been a pot of wilting geraniums.

He went back home looking like a drowned rat, worn out from fatigue and hunger, and since he no longer had the strength to stand, he sat down, resting his soaked and muddy feet on the brazier, still full of live coals.

He fell asleep. And as he slept, his wooden feet caught fire and slowly burnt away until they were nothing but ash.

Pinocchio slept through it all, snoring, as if they were someone else's feet. Finally he woke, at dawn, when someone knocked at the door.

"Who is it?" he asked, yawning and rubbing his hands together.

"It's me!" a voice replied.

That voice was the voice of Geppetto.

Chapter 7

Poor Pinocchio: he was still half asleep and hadn't yet noticed that his feet had burnt right off. That's why, when he heard his father's voice, he leapt off his stool to run and unbolt the door. Instead, he lurched this way and that, and then he tumbled headlong to the ground.

When he hit the floor he made the same sound that a sack of wooden spoons might make if dropped off a tall building.

Meanwhile Geppetto was shouting, "Open up!"

"I can't, Daddy," replied the puppet as he wept and flailed.

"Why can't you?"

"Because my feet got eaten!"

"And who ate them?"

"The cat," said Pinocchio, noticing that the cat was amusing itself by batting wood shavings with its forepaws.

"Open up, I say!" said Geppetto again. "Or else when I get in I'll eat you myself!"

"I can't stand up, believe me. Oh, poor me, poor me! I'll have to walk on my knees for the rest of my life!"

Thinking that all this whining was just another of the puppet's pranks, Geppetto decided to put a stop to it. He climbed the wall and went in through the window.

He was ready to say and do certain things, but when he saw that his Pinocchio, sprawled there on the ground, really had lost his feet, his heart melted. He took him in his arms at once and began kissing and stroking him and whispering a thousand tender words and sobbing, and as shiny tears ran down his cheeks, he said, "My darling Pinocchio! How in the world did you burn your feet off?"

"I don't know, Daddy, but it was such a dreadful night and I'll remember it for the rest of my days. There was thunder and lightening, and I was famished, and then the Talking Cricket said to me, 'Serves you right, you've been naughty, you deserve it,' and I said, 'Watch out, Cricket!' and he said, 'You're a puppet and you're a blockhead,' and I threw a wooden mallet at him, and he died, but it was his fault, because I didn't want to kill him, the proof being that I put a little skillet on the live coals of the brazier, but the Chick

Chapter 8

No sooner had the puppet satisfied his hunger than he began grousing and crying, because he wanted a pair of new feet.

But Geppetto, as punishment for his pranks, let him cry and despair for half a day, then said, "And why should I make you new feet? So I can see you run away from home again?"

"I promise," said the sobbing puppet, "that from now on I'll be good."

"That's what all children say," replied Geppetto, "when they're trying to get something."

"I promise I'll go to school, I'll study, I'll make you proud."

"These are the very things all children say when they're trying to get something."

"But I'm not like other children! I'm better than the rest, and I always tell the truth. I promise you, Daddy, that I'll learn a trade, and that I'll be the staff and comfort of your old age."

Geppetto was trying to look severe, but his eyes brimmed with tears and his heart swelled with compassion at seeing his poor Pinocchio in such a pitiful state. Without another word, he took up the tools of his trade, along with two pieces of seasoned wood, and he set to work in great earnest.

In less than an hour, the two little feet were finished, and they were as nimble, lean, and sinewy as if they had been fashioned by a brilliant artist.

Geppetto then told the puppet, "Close your eyes and go to sleep!"

And so Pinocchio closed his eyes and pretended to sleep. Meanwhile, Geppetto stuck the new feet in place with some glue he had melted in an eggshell, and he stuck them on so well that you couldn't even see the joint.

As soon as the puppet realized the feet were on, he jumped down from the table where he had been lying and began skipping and capering about the room as if driven crazy by so much happiness.

"To repay you for everything you've done for me," said Pinocchio to his daddy, "I want to go to school right away."

"Good boy."

"But before I can go to school, I need clothes."

Geppetto, who was poor and didn't have so much as a penny in his pocket, fashioned a humble outfit out of flowered paper, a pair of shoes out of tree bark, and a new cap out of breadcrumbs.

Pinocchio ran to look at himself in a basin full of water, and he was so pleased with what he saw that he began strutting like a peacock, saying, "I look like a real gentleman!"

"It's true," replied Geppetto, "because it isn't fine clothes, you must remember, that make a gentlemen – it's clean clothes."

"By the way," continued the puppet, "there's one more thing I need before I can go to school – in fact, the best and most important thing of all."

"What's that?"

"I need a spelling book."

"You're right, but how can we get one?"

"Simple: we go to a bookseller and buy one."

"What about money?"

"I don't have any."

"Me neither," added the kind old man, growing sad.

And Pinocchio, though he was a very cheerful boy, grew sad, too, because poverty, if it's true poverty, is understood by everyone, even children.

"Don't worry!" shouted Geppetto, suddenly springing to his feet. He put on his old fustian coat, all patches and darnings, and ran out of the door.

He soon returned, and when he came in the door he had his son's spelling book in his hands, but no coat. The poor man was in shirtsleeves, though it was snowing outside.

"Where's your coat, Daddy?"

"I sold it."

"Why did you sell it?"

"Because I was hot."

Pinocchio quickly grasped what his answer meant, and he couldn't resist the good-hearted impulse to throw his arms around Geppetto's neck and begin covering his face with kisses.

Chapter 9

As soon as it stopped snowing, Pinocchio, with his nifty new spelling book tucked under his arm, set out down the road to school. Along the way, his little brain dreamt up a thousand things, a thousand castles in the air, each more lovely than the last.

Conversing with himself, he said, "Today, at school, I'll quickly learn to read; then tomorrow I'll learn to write; and the day after tomorrow I'll learn my numbers. Then, with all that knowledge, I'll make a lot of money, and with the first money that comes into my hands I'll buy my daddy a fine wool coat. But what am I saying, 'wool'? I'll buy him a coat made of silver and gold, with diamond buttons. And that poor man truly deserves it – because, after all, in order to buy me books and send me to school, he's going around in shirtsleeves. In this cold! There are some sacrifices only a father would make!"

In the midst of all this emotional talk, he thought he heard, in the distance, the music of fifes and the beats of a big drum: *dee-dee-dee, dee-dee-dee, dum, dum, dum, dum.*

He stopped to listen. Those sounds came from the end of a long side road that led to a tiny little village constructed by the seaside.

"What could that music be? It's too bad I have to go to school, otherwise . . ."

And there he stood, uncertain. One thing was sure: he had to do something, either go to school or listen to the fifes.

"Today I'll go to hear the fifes, tomorrow I'll go to school – there's always time for school," the rascal finally said, shrugging his shoulders.

Wasting no time, he headed down the side road and soon was running at top speed. The more he ran, the clearer he heard the sound of the fifes and the thumps of the big drum: *dee-dee-dee, dee-dee-dee, dee-dee-dee, dum, dum, dum, dum.*

Suddenly he found himself in the middle of a square packed with people. They were crowding around a big wooden booth covered with canvas that was painted with a thousand colours.

Turning to a little local boy, Pinocchio asked, "What is that booth?"

"It's written on that poster. Read it and you'll know."

"I'd gladly read it, but it just so happens that I can't read today."

"Bravo, dummy! OK, I'll read it to you. For your information, those fire-red letters on the poster say: *Great Puppet Show.*"

"How long ago did the show start?"

"It's starting now."

"And how much does it cost to get in?"

"Twenty pennies."

Pinocchio, in a fever of curiosity, lost all self-control and shamelessly asked the boy, "Would you loan me twenty pennies until tomorrow?"

"I'd gladly give them to you," said the boy, mocking him, "but it just so happens that I can't today."

"I'd sell you my jacket for twenty pennies," the puppet said to the boy.

"What am I supposed to do with a jacket made of flowery paper? If I got rained on, I'd never get it off."

"You want to buy my shoes?"

"They'd be good for lighting fires."

"How much will you give me for my hat?"

"Now that would be a bargain! A breadcrumb hat! Maybe the mice would come eat it off my head!"

Pinocchio was on tenterhooks. He was just about to make one last offer, but he couldn't bring himself to do it. He hemmed and hawed, he shilly-shallied, he agonized. At last he said, "Would you give me twenty pennies for this new spelling book?"

"I'm just a child, and I don't buy things from other children," replied his little interlocutor, who had more sense than Pinocchio did.

"For twenty pennies, I'll buy that spelling book," cried a rag-picker who happened to be listening to their conversation.

The book was sold right then and there. And to think that poor Geppetto was sitting at home shivering in shirtsleeves from the cold just so his son could have a spelling book!

Chapter 10

When Pinocchio entered the puppet theatre, something happened that triggered a small revolution.

It's important to understand that the curtain had been raised and the play had already begun.

Onstage, Harlequin and Punchinello were already quarrelling with each other, as usual, and threatening at any moment to exchange a barrage of slaps and blows.

The audience was riveted, and they laughed till their bellies ached at the bickering of those two puppets, who gesticulated and traded insults so realistically that they truly appeared to be two thinking beings, two persons of this world.

Then all of a sudden, out of the blue, Harlequin stopped acting, turned towards the audience, pointed towards someone in the back of the pit, and started yelling in dramatic tones: "Good heavens! Do I dream or am I awake? Yet surely I see, there in the back, Pinocchio!"

"It truly is Pinocchio!" shouted Punchinello.

"It's really him!" squealed Miss Rosaura, peeping out from the back of the stage.

"It's Pinocchio! It's Pinocchio!" all the puppets screamed in unison, leaping out from the wings. "It's Pinocchio! It's our brother, Pinocchio! Long live Pinocchio!"

"Pinocchio, come up here where I am!" shouted Harlequin. "Come throw yourself into the arms of your wooden brothers!"

At this affectionate invitation, Pinocchio leapt from the back of the pit into the expensive seats, then jumped again from the expensive seats onto the orchestra conductor's head, and then sprang from there onto the stage.

You can't imagine all the hugging and embracing, the friendly pinches and the sincere head butts of brotherhood that Pinocchio received amid this mayhem from the actors and actresses of that plant-kingdom troupe.

It was a heartwarming spectacle, no doubt. But the audience, seeing that the play had ground to a halt, grew impatient and began to shout, "We want the play, we want the play!"

They were wasting their breath, because the puppets, instead of going on with the show,

redoubled their rumpus and fuss, hoisting Pinocchio onto their shoulders and carrying him triumphantly into the footlights.

It was then that the puppet master came out, an enormous man, and so ugly that the mere sight of him was frightening. His foul beard was black as an inkblot and so long that it dragged on the ground. Let's just say he stepped on it when he walked. His mouth was as wide as an oven, his eyes were like lanterns whose flames shone through panes of red glass, and his hands were cracking a big whip, made of snakes and foxtails braided together.

At the unexpected appearance of the puppet master, the crowd fell silent, holding its breath. You could have heard a pin drop. Those poor puppets, male and female alike, trembled like so many leaves.

"Why are you causing such a commotion in my theatre?" the puppet master asked Pinocchio, booming like an ogre with a bad cold.

"Believe me, kind sir, it wasn't my fault!"

"That's enough out of you! We'll settle this business tonight."

Indeed, as soon as the play was finished, the puppet master went into the kitchen, where he was fixing himself a nice big ram for dinner; it turned slowly on a spit over the fire. But since he didn't have enough wood to finish browning it, he called in Harlequin and Punchinello and said, "Fetch me that puppet – you'll find him hanging on a nail. I think he's made of good, dry wood, and I'm sure that if I toss him on the fire, it will flare up nicely and finish the roasting."

At first, Harlequin and Punchinello hesitated. But then, afraid of incurring their owner's wrath, they obeyed. They soon returned to the kitchen, carrying poor Pinocchio, who was wriggling like an eel out of water and screaming helplessly: "Oh save me, Daddy! I don't want to die! No, I don't want to die!"

Chapter 11

I won't deny it: Fire-Eater (this was the puppet master's name) did indeed look scary, with that foul black beard of his that covered his chest and legs like an apron. But deep down he really wasn't a bad man. In fact, when he saw poor Pinocchio brought before him, struggling every which way and howling, "I don't want to die, I don't want to die!" he was immediately moved to pity. He resisted the feeling for quite some time, but finally he could no longer help himself: he let out a resounding sneeze.

Before that sneeze, Harlequin had looked hopelessly sad and was hunched over like a weeping willow. But after it, his face lit up and, leaning towards Pinocchio, he whispered, "Good news, brother! The puppet master sneezed, and that means he feels sorry for you, so you'll be OK now."

It's important to know that while most people cry when they feel sorry for someone, or at least make a show of wiping their eyes, Fire-Eater was in the habit, when deeply moved, of sneezing. It was as good a way as any to show other people what he felt in his heart.

After sneezing, the puppet master, still grumpy, yelled at Pinocchio: "Stop that crying! Your wailing is giving me such a bellyache, causing me such cramps, it's almost – *ah-choo! ah-choo!*"

"Bless you!" said Pinocchio.

"Thank you," said Fire-Eater. "And your father and mother, are they still alive?"

"My daddy is. I never knew my mother."

"I can only imagine what a blow it would be for your old father if I had you thrown onto those burning coals! That poor old man! I feel sorry – *ah-choo! ah-choo! ah-choo!*"

"Bless you!" said Pinocchio.

"Thank you! On the other hand, you should feel sorry for me, too, since as you can see I don't have enough wood to finish roasting this ram; the fact is you really would have come in handy right about now. But I've already taken pity on you, so that's that. Instead, I'll put one of the puppets from my troupe onto the coals beneath that spit. Oh, guards!"

At this command, two wooden guards appeared at once. Both were very tall and very thin, with Napoleon hats on their heads and unsheathed swords in their hands.

Then the puppet master, his voice hoarse, said to them, "Fetch me Harlequin there, tie him up good, then throw him onto that fire. I want my ram well roasted!"

Just imagine how poor Harlequin felt! So frightened was he that his knees buckled and he fell forwards onto the ground.

At this heartrending sight, Pinocchio threw himself at the puppet master's feet, weeping copiously and bathing that long beard in his tears. He began to speak in pleading tones: "Have mercy, kind sir!"

"There are no sirs here!" growled the puppet master.

"Have mercy, noble knight!"

"There are no knights here!"

"Have mercy, my lord!"

"There are no lords here!"

"Have mercy, Your Excellency!"

Hearing himself called Excellency, the puppet master quickly pursed his lips and, having suddenly become gentler and more agreeable, he said to Pinocchio, "Well then, what is it you want from me?"

"I implore you to have mercy on poor Harlequin!"

"This is no time for mercy. If I save you, it means I have to put him on the fire, because I want that ram of mine to be well roasted."

"In that case," cried Pinocchio proudly, standing and throwing off his breadcrumb cap, "in that case, I know what I must do. Come, guards! Tie me up and throw me into those flames. No, it isn't fair for poor Harlequin, my true friend, to die in my place."

At these words, pronounced loudly and heroically, every puppet in the room burst into tears. Even the guards, though made of wood, cried like a pair of newborn lambs.

Fire-Eater, at first, remained as hard and firm as a block of ice. But then, little by little, he too began melting and sneezing. After sneezing four or five times, he opened his arms warmly to Pinocchio and said, "You are a marvellously good boy! Come here and give me a kiss."

Pinocchio ran over to the puppet master, clambered like a squirrel up his beard, and planted a big kiss on the tip of his nose.

"Then mercy is granted?" asked poor Harlequin, in a feeble voice the others could barely hear.

"Mercy is granted!" replied Fire-Eater. And then, sighing and shaking his head, he added: "That's that! Tonight I'll have to make do with half-raw mutton. But beware: next time it will be someone else's turn!"

Hearing that mercy had been granted, the puppets all ran to the stage, lit the lamps and chandeliers as if for a gala performance, and began to leap and dance about. When dawn arrived, they were dancing still.

Chapter 12

The next day Fire-Eater took Pinocchio aside and asked him, "What's your father's name?"

"Geppetto."

"And what's his trade?"

"Being poor."

"Does he earn much?"

"He earns enough never to have a penny in his pocket. Why, just to buy me a spelling book for school, he had to sell his one and only coat, which was so covered with patches it looked like it had the plague."

"The poor devil! I nearly feel sorry for him. Here are five gold pieces – take them to him at once, along with my warmest wishes."

Pinocchio, as you can imagine, thanked the puppet master a thousand times. He hugged every puppet in the company, one by one – even the guards. And then, beside himself with joy, he set out for home.

But he had not walked half a kilometre when he met a Fox, who was lame in one leg, and a Cat, who was blind in both eyes. They were helping each other slowly down the road, like good companions in misfortune. The Fox, being lame, was leaning on the Cat, and the Cat, being blind, was following the Fox.

"Good day, Pinocchio," said the Fox, greeting him politely.

"How is it that you know my name?" asked the puppet.

"I know your father well."

"Where did you see him last?"

"I saw him yesterday at the door of his house."

"What was he doing?"

"He was in shirtsleeves and was shivering from the cold."

"My poor daddy! But, God willing, he won't be shivering after today."

"Why not?"

"Because I've become a rich man."

"A rich man – you?" said the Fox, breaking into crude, derisive laughter. The Cat was also laughing, a fact he tried to hide by grooming his whiskers with his forepaws.

"It's nothing to laugh at," cried Pinocchio, crossly. "I apologize in advance for making your mouths water, but these here, in case you didn't know, are five fabulous gold pieces." And out of his pocket he pulled the coins Fire-Eater had given him.

Hearing the pleasant sound those coins made, the Fox reached out, in an involuntary motion, the leg that had seemed lame, and the Cat opened his eyes, which shone like two green lanterns, before closing them again so quickly that Pinocchio didn't notice a thing.

"And now," asked the Fox, "just what do you plan to do with those coins?"

"First of all," the puppet replied, "I'll buy my daddy a brand-new coat, made of gold and silver and with diamond buttons, and then I'll get a spelling book for myself."

"For yourself?"

"Indeed. Because I want to go to school and be a good student."

"But look at me!" said the Fox. "Thanks to a foolish enthusiasm for studying, I lost the use of one leg!"

"And look at me!" said the Cat. "Thanks to a foolish enthusiasm for studying, I lost the use of both eyes!"

Just then a white Blackbird, perched on a hedge beside the road, whistled his usual tune and said, "Pinocchio, pay no mind to the advice of bad companions – you'll be sorry if you do!"

Poor Blackbird – if only he had said nothing! The Cat leapt high in the air and pounced on him, swallowing him whole, feathers and all, before he could even say "ouch!"

As soon as he had finished eating and cleaned his mouth, the Cat shut his eyes once more and went back to being blind.

"Poor Blackbird!" said Pinocchio to the Cat. "Why were you so mean to him?"

"To teach him a lesson. Next time he'll know better than to stick his beak into other people's business."

They were more than halfway to Geppetto's house when the Fox, stopping suddenly, said to the puppet, "Want to double your money?"

"Meaning?"

"Do you want to take five measly gold coins and turn them into a hundred, a thousand, two thousand?"

"Sure! But how?"

"Simple as can be: instead of going straight home, come with us."

"And where do you propose to take me?"

"To the Land of Gulls."

Pinocchio thought on this for a moment before replying firmly, "No, I don't want to come. I'm almost back home now, and I want to see my daddy, who's waiting for me. Who knows how much that poor old man worried yesterday, when I didn't return. Unfortunately, I've been a bad boy. The Talking Cricket was right when he said that disobedient children will come to no good in this world, and I've learned the hard way, by getting into lots of trouble, and just last night at Fire-Eater's house, I was in such danger – *brrr!* I get goose bumps just thinking about it!"

"So," said the Fox, "you really want to go back home? Go ahead, then. It's your loss."

"Your loss!" repeated the Cat.

"Think it over, Pinocchio – you're turning your back on fortune."

"On fortune!" repeated the Cat.

"Your five gold coins could become two thousand overnight."

"Overnight!" repeated the Cat.

"But how could they possibly become so much?" asked Pinocchio, his mouth hanging open in astonishment.

"I'll explain at once," said the Fox. "You must know that in the Land of Gulls there is a sacred field that everybody calls the Field of Miracles. You dig a hole in this field and you put something, a gold coin for example, into the hole. Then you cover it up with a little earth, water it with two bucketfuls of springwater, sprinkle it with a pinch of salt, and when evening comes you go happily to bed. While you're sleeping, the coin will sprout and flower, and the next morning when you get up and go back to the field, what will you find? You'll find a big tree laden with as many gold coins as there are kernels on a good ear of corn in the month of June."

"So," said Pinocchio, increasingly amazed, "if I buried my five gold pieces in that field, how many would I find the next morning?"

"That's easily determined," replied the Fox. "You can count it out on your fingers. Let's say that each coin grows into a bunch of five hundred coins – multiply five hundred by five, and the next morning you'd have two thousand five hundred shiny new coins."

"How wonderful!" shouted Pinocchio, jumping with joy. "As soon as I've gathered up all those coins, I'll keep two thousand for myself and I'll give the other five hundred as a gift to you two."

"A gift to us?" shouted the Fox, taking offence and looking hurt. "God forbid!"

"Forbid!" repeated the Cat.

"We," continued the Fox, "do not work for selfish reasons. We work solely to enrich others."

"Others!" repeated the Cat.

"What nice people," thought Pinocchio to himself. And he forgot, on the spot, about his father, the new coat, his spelling book – about all the resolutions he had made – and he said to the Fox and the Cat, "Let's get started right now, I'm coming with you."

Chapter 13

They walked and walked and walked, and at dusk they finally arrived, dead tired, at the Red Crayfish Inn.

"Let's stop here a while," said the Fox, "to get a bite to eat and rest for a few hours. Then we'll set out again at midnight, so as to reach the Field of Miracles by dawn."

They entered the inn and sat down at a table, but none of them had any appetite.

The poor Cat, due to a terribly upset stomach, managed to eat only thirty-five goatfish in red sauce and four portions of tripe parmesan. And finding the tripe insufficiently seasoned, he called for more butter and grated cheese – three times!

The Fox, too, would have gladly nibbled on something, but since his doctor had put him on an extra-strict diet, he had to content himself with a simple hare in soursweet sauce, along with a tiny side order of fat pullets and fine cockerels. After the hare, to clear his palate, he ordered a goulash of partridges, quails, rabbits, frogs, lizards, and paradise grapes – and that was simply all he could eat. Food made him so sick to his stomach, he said, that he could barely stand to look at it.

But Pinocchio ate least of all. He ordered half a walnut and a crust of bread, but even those items were left on his plate. The poor boy couldn't stop thinking about the Field of Miracles, and all those gold coins gave him indigestion in advance.

When they had finished supper, the Fox said to the innkeeper, "Give me two good rooms, one for Mr Pinocchio and the other for my companion and myself. We'll take a little nap before we leave. But don't forget to wake us at midnight so that we may continue on our journey."

"Yessir," replied the innkeeper, winking at the Fox and the Cat as if to say: *I catch your drift and we're on the same page.*

No sooner had Pinocchio climbed into bed than he fell fast asleep and began to dream. He dreamt he was in the middle of a field, and this field was full of trees laden with clusters of fruit, like grapes, but in the place of grapes were gold coins, which clinked and chimed in the breeze as if to say, "Whoever wants us, come and get us." But in the very moment when Pinocchio was reaching up, ready to grab handfuls of those lovely coins and stuff them in his pockets, he was awoken by three thundering knocks on the door of his room.

It was the innkeeper, come to tell him that the clock had struck midnight.

"Are my companions ready to go?" the puppet asked.

"More than ready! They left two hours ago."

"What was the rush?"

"The Cat received a message saying that his oldest kitten was suffering from chilblains and was at death's door."

"Did they pay for supper?"

"What do you think? They're too polite to insult a gentleman such as yourself in that fashion."

"What a shame – I wouldn't mind being insulted in that fashion!" Pinocchio said, scratching his head. Then he asked, "And where did those dear friends of mine say I should meet them?"

"At the Field of Miracles, at the break of day."

Pinocchio gave the innkeeper one of his gold coins to cover his dinner and that of his companions, and then he set out.

But you might say he had to grope his way forwards: it was so dark outside the inn that he couldn't see his hand in front of his face. Nor could he hear, in the surrounding countryside, so much as the rustling of a leaf – except for the ominous night birds that occasionally flapped their wings against Pinocchio's nose as they flew across the road from one hedge to the other. Each time, Pinocchio jumped back, afraid, and shouted, "Who goes there?" And the surrounding hills sent back a distant, repeating echo: *Who-goes-there? Who-goes-there? Who-goes-there?*

At one point during his walk, he saw, on a tree trunk, a small creature that glowed with a pale, dull light, like a translucent porcelain night lamp with a tiny flame burning inside.

"Who are you?" said the puppet.

"I'm the ghost of the Talking Cricket," replied the creature in the faintest of voices, which seemed to come from the world beyond.

"What do you want with me?"

"I want to give you some advice. Turn around and take your four remaining gold coins straight to your poor father, who is weeping and despairing because you haven't come home."

"Tomorrow my daddy will be a great gentleman, because I'm going to turn these four gold pieces into two thousand."

"My boy, never trust those who promise to make you rich overnight. They're usually either madmen or swindlers! Take my advice and turn back."

"But I want to keep going."

"The hour is late!"

"I want to keep going."

"The night is dark!"

"I want to keep going."

"The road is perilous!"

"I want to keep going."

"Remember that children who want to do everything their way come sooner or later to regret it!"

"Same old story. Good night, Cricket."

"Good night, Pinocchio. May heaven protect you from morning dew and murderers."

No sooner had he uttered these words than the Talking Cricket vanished, like a candle someone had blown out, leaving the street even darker than before.

Chapter 14

"It's amazing," said the puppet to himself as he resumed his journey, "how unlucky we poor children are! Everyone scolds us, everyone warns us, everyone gives us advice. They seem to have got the notion, to hear them talk, that they're both our fathers and our teachers, every last one of them, even talking crickets. And just because I didn't follow that dreary Cricket's advice, he tells me that all sorts of bad things will happen to me! Supposedly I'll even run into murderers! It's a good thing I don't believe in murderers – never have. In my opinion, murderers were made up by fathers just to scare kids who wanted to go out at night. And besides, even if I did meet some on the road, you think I'd be afraid of them? Not a chance. I'd go right up to them and shout, 'Hey, Mr Murderers, what do you want with me? You better not try any funny stuff! Just run along and mind your own business!' I can see it now: at that torrent of harsh words, those murderers would run like the wind. And if they happened to be rude enough not to run away, well then, I'd run away myself, and that would be the end . . ."

But Pinocchio was unable to finish his train of thought, because just at that moment he thought he heard a slight rustling of leaves behind him.

He turned to look, and there, in the dark, he saw two ominous black figures, completely draped in coal sacks. They were bounding towards him on tiptoe, like ghosts.

"They really do exist!" he thought, and not knowing where else to hide his four gold coins, he stuck them into his mouth, under his tongue.

Then he tried to escape. But before he had taken a single step, his arms were seized and he heard two horrible, cavernous voices saying, "Your money or your life!"

Since the coins in his mouth prevented him from responding with words, Pinocchio made a thousand faces and gestures, like a mime, in an attempt to make it clear to those two hooded figures – whose eyes were all he could see, through holes in the sacks – that he was a poor puppet without so much as a phony penny to his name.

"Come on! Cut the act and give us the money!" shouted the murderers in menacing tones.

And the puppet made a gesture with his head and his hands, as if to say: "I don't have any."

"Hand over the money or you're dead!" said the tall one.

"Dead!" said the short one.

"And after we kill you, we'll kill your daddy, too!"

"Your daddy, too!"

"No, no, no, not my poor daddy!" yelled Pinocchio, desperation in his voice. But when he yelled, the gold pieces clinked in his mouth.

"Oh, you rascal! So you've hidden the money under your tongue? Spit it out, right now!" But Pinocchio refused!

"What, are you deaf? Just you wait, we'll make you spit it out!"

At that, one of them seized the puppet by the tip of his nose and the other grabbed hold of his pointed chin, and they began tugging, quite rudely, in opposite directions, trying to force the puppet's mouth open – but to no avail. It was as if his mouth had been nailed and riveted shut.

Then one of the murderers, the short one, whipped out a nasty-looking knife and tried to stick it between Pinocchio's lips, like a lever or chisel. But Pinocchio, quick as lightning, chomped down on the hand with his teeth, bit it clean off, and spat it out. Imagine his astonishment when he looked at the ground and saw he had bitten off not a hand but a cat's paw.

Emboldened by this first victory of his, he wrenched himself free from the murderers' clutches, jumped over the roadside hedge, and fled into the countryside. And the murderers followed, like two dogs after a rabbit. And the one who had lost a paw ran on a single leg – no one ever knew how he managed it.

After running fifteen kilometers, Pinocchio couldn't go any farther. As a last-ditch effort, he climbed up the trunk of a towering pine tree and sat in the topmost branches. The murderers tried to climb the tree, too, but halfway up they slipped and slid back down to the ground, skinning their hands and feet.

Instead of giving up, they piled dry sticks around the base of the tree and set them on fire. In no time, the pine began to burn and blaze like a candle in the breeze. Seeing the flames rise higher and higher and not wanting to end up like a roasted pigeon, Pinocchio made a great leap from the top of the tree and began running again through fields and vineyards. The murderers gave chase and kept chasing, never tiring.

Day was beginning to break, with the murderers still in pursuit, when Pinocchio found his path blocked by an enormous ditch full of filthy water that was the muddy colour of coffee with milk. What was he to do? "One, two, three!" yelled the puppet, and with a running start he leapt to the opposite bank. The murderers jumped, too, but not having judged the distance properly, they fell – *kersplash!* – smack in the middle of the ditch. When Pinocchio heard them flailing in the water, he shouted through his laughter, "Enjoy your bath, Mr Murderers!" And he kept on running.

He was imagining them nicely drowned, but when he turned round to look, he saw that they were both still chasing him, still draped in their coal sacks, gushing water like a pair of upside-down baskets.

Chapter 15

Just as the puppet, terribly discouraged, was on the point of flinging himself to the ground and giving up, he happened to look round and see, through the dark green of the trees, a little white house, gleaming in the distance like snow.

"If only I had strength enough to reach that house, perhaps I would be saved!" he thought.

Not wasting a moment, he started running at full speed again, towards the forest. The murderers were still behind him.

At last, after racing desperately for almost two hours, he arrived, completely out of breath, at the door of the little house, and he knocked.

No answer.

He knocked again, harder this time, for he could hear the rapid approach of footsteps and the loud, panting breath of his persecutors. Still no answer.

In desperation, since knocking wasn't working, he began to kick the door and bang his head against it. Then a beautiful girl came to the window, her hair sky-blue, her face white as a waxen image. Her eyes were closed and her hands were folded across her chest, and without moving her lips she said, in a tiny voice that seemed to come from the world beyond, "There is no one in this house. They are all dead."

"Open the door yourself, at least!" begged Pinocchio, weeping.

"I too am dead."

"Dead? But then what are you doing there at the window?"

"I am waiting for the coffin to come and carry me away."

As soon as she had uttered those words, the girl disappeared, and the window closed again without a sound.

"Oh, Beautiful Girl with Sky-Blue Hair," yelled Pinocchio, "for pity's sake open the door! Have mercy on a poor boy chased by murd—"

But he was unable to finish the word, for he felt himself being seized by the neck, and he heard two familiar voices growl menacingly: "You won't get away again!"

The puppet, seeing death flashing before his eyes, trembled so hard that the joints of his wooden legs and the four gold coins hidden beneath his tongue all rattled.

"Well then," the murderers asked him, "will you open your mouth or not? What, no reply?

Never mind, this time we'll make you open it!"

They each whipped out a nasty-looking knife, long and razor sharp, and stabbed him – *whack, whack* – right in the back.

Luckily, the puppet was made of very hard wood indeed, which explains why both blades shattered into a thousand pieces, leaving the murderers holding only the handles of their knives and gaping at each other.

"I know," said the tall one, "we have to hang him! Let's hang him!"

"Hang him!" repeated the short one.

They wasted no time tying his hands behind his back and slipping a noose over his head, and then they strung him up from a branch of a large tree called the Big Oak.

And then they waited, sitting on the grass below, for the puppet to stop kicking. But after three hours, his eyes were still open, his mouth still closed, and he was kicking more than ever.

Finally, tired of waiting, they turned to Pinocchio and sneered: "Goodbye until tomorrow. When we come back, let's hope you'll be so kind as to let us find you good and dead, with that mouth of yours wide open."

And off they went.

Soon a violent north wind blew in, raging and howling and jerking the poor dangling puppet this way and that, making him swing as wildly as the clapper of a church bell on Sunday. The swinging caused him terrible pain, and the noose grew ever tighter, cutting off his breath.

Little by little, his eyes grew dim, and though he felt himself approaching death, he continued to hope that at any moment some merciful soul might yet come to his aid. But when, after waiting and waiting, he saw that no one was coming, no one at all, then he thought of his poor father – and there at death's door he stammered, "Oh, if only you were here, Daddy!"

He lacked the strength to say another word. His eyes closed, his mouth opened, his legs straightened, and then, after a tremendous shudder, he went completely limp.

Chapter 16

Poor Pinocchio: having been hung by murderers from a branch of the Big Oak, he now seemed more dead than alive. When the Beautiful Girl with Sky-Blue Hair came to her window again, she was moved to pity by the sight of that poor wretch, dangling by his neck, dancing a jig with the north wind. She brought her hands together three times, making three soft claps.

Her signal was followed by a great beating of wings, as an enormous falcon hurtled down from the sky and landed on the windowsill.

"What is your command, my lovely Fairy?" said the Falcon, lowering his beak in a gesture of reverence. (For it just so happened that the Girl with Sky-Blue Hair was none other than the kindest of fairies, one who had dwelt in and around that forest for more than a thousand years.)

"Do you see that puppet dangling from a branch of the Big Oak?"

"I see him."

"Now then: fly to him at once, use your powerful beak to tear apart the knot that keeps him suspended in the air, and lay him out gently on the grass, there at the foot of the tree."

The Falcon flew off and two minutes later returned, saying, "I have done as you commanded."

"And how did you find him: alive or dead?"

"He looked dead at first, but he must not be thoroughly dead, because as soon as I loosened the rope around his neck, he sighed and murmured, 'I feel better now!'"

Then the Fairy brought her hands together twice, making two soft claps, and suddenly a magnificent poodle appeared, and he was walking on his hind legs just as people do.

The Poodle was dressed as a coachman, in the finest livery. He wore a tricorn hat with gold-braid trim, a white wig of curly locks that hung down to his shoulders, a chocolate-coloured jacket with diamond buttons and two oversized pockets for storing the bones his mistress gave him at dinner, a pair of crimson velvet breeches, silk stockings, little court shoes, and, behind him, a sort of umbrella cover, made entirely of sky-blue satin, that he put over his tail in rainy weather.

"Be a good boy, Lancelot," said the Fairy to the Poodle, "and go harness the finest carriage in my carriage house and take the forest road to the Big Oak. There you'll find a poor puppet stretched out half dead on the grass. Pick him up gently, lay him ever so carefully on the cushions inside the carriage, and bring him here to me. Do you understand?"

The Poodle wagged the sky-blue satin cover three or four times, to show that he understood, and then raced off like a Barbary steed.

Out of the carriage house, moments later, there came a beautiful little sky-coloured carriage, padded with canary-feathered cushions and lined with whipped cream, custard, and ladyfingers. It was drawn by a hundred pairs of white mice, and the Poodle, up on the driver's seat, was cracking his whip from side to side, like someone who's afraid he's running late.

In less than a quarter of an hour, the little carriage was back. The Fairy, waiting at the door of the house, took the poor puppet in her arms and carried him into a small room with mother-of-pearl walls. Then she quickly sent for the most famous doctors in the area.

The doctors soon arrived, one after the other. The first was a crow, the second an owl, and the third a talking cricket.

"I would like you gentlemen to tell me," said the Fairy, looking at the three doctors gathered around Pinocchio's bed, "I would like you gentlemen to tell me whether this unlucky puppet is alive or dead!"

Hearing this request, the Crow stepped forwards first. He felt Pinocchio's pulse, then he felt his nose, then he felt his little toe, and when he had finished feeling all these things very carefully, he solemnly pronounced these words: "It is my opinion that the puppet is quite dead. But if by some strange chance he is not dead, then that would be a sure sign that he is still alive."

"I regret," said the Owl, "that I must contradict my illustrious friend and colleague, the Crow. I believe, rather, that the puppet is still alive. But if by some strange chance he is not alive, then that would indicate that he is, in fact, dead."

"And you – do you have nothing to say?" the Fairy asked the Talking Cricket.

"I say that the best thing a prudent doctor can do when he doesn't know what he's talking about is to keep his mouth shut. And as for that puppet there, his countenance is not new to me – I've known him for some time!"

Pinocchio had been lying motionless, like a true piece of wood, but at these words he began shuddering feverishly, causing the whole bed to shake.

"That puppet there," continued the Talking Cricket, "is a confirmed rogue."

Pinocchio opened his eyes and quickly shut them again.

"He's a ragamuffin, a lazybones, a vagabond."

Pinocchio hid his face beneath the sheets.

"That puppet there is a disobedient brat who will cause his poor father to die of a heart attack!"

Now everyone in the room could hear the muffled sound of crying and sobbing. Imagine their reaction when, after peering under the sheets, they realized that those cries and sobs were coming from Pinocchio.

"When a dead person cries, it's a sign that he's on the mend," said the Crow solemnly.

"It grieves me to contradict my illustrious friend and colleague," added the Owl, "but I believe that when a dead person cries, it's a sign that he doesn't like dying."

Chapter 17

As soon as the three doctors had left the room, the Fairy went to Pinocchio's side and discovered, by touching his forehead, that he was suffering from a terribly high fever. She then dissolved a special white powder in half a glass of water and offered it to the puppet, saying lovingly, "Drink it, and in a few days you will be cured."

Pinocchio looked at the glass, scrunched up his mouth, and then asked in a whiny voice: "Is it sweet or bitter?"

"It's bitter, but it will do you good."

"If it's bitter, I don't want it."

"Listen to me: drink it."

"I don't like bitter stuff."

"Drink it – and after you do, I'll give you a lump of sugar, to take away the bitterness."

"Where's the lump of sugar?"

"Right here," said the Fairy, extracting one from a gold sugar bowl.

"First I want the lump of sugar, and then I'll choke down that bitter stuff."

"Promise?"

"Yes."

As soon as the Fairy handed him the lump of sugar, Pinocchio chewed it up and gulped it down. Licking his lips, he said, "Wouldn't it be great if sugar was medicine, too? I'd take some every day."

"Now keep your promise and drink these few drops, which will restore you to health."

Pinocchio reluctantly took the glass from her hand and stuck the tip of his nose in it. Then he brought it up to his lips.

But in the end he said, "It's too bitter! too bitter! I can't drink it."

"How can you say that if you haven't even tasted it?"

"I can tell! I smelt it. First I want another lump of sugar – then I'll drink it!"

And so, with all the patience of a good mother, the Fairy put a little more sugar in his mouth. Then she gave him the glass again.

"I can't drink it like this!" said the puppet, making all kinds of faces.

"Why not?"

"Because that pillow down there on my feet is bothering me."

The Fairy removed the pillow.

"It's no use! I still can't bear to drink it."

"What else is bothering you?"

"The door to this room – it's open."

The Fairy went and closed the door.

"The fact is," yelled Pinocchio, bursting into tears, "I just won't drink this nasty bitter stuff – I won't, I won't, I won't!"

"You'll be sorry, my boy."

"I don't care."

"You're terribly ill."

"I don't care."

"In a few hours the fever will carry you to the world beyond."

"I don't care."

"You're not afraid of death?"

"Not at all! I'd rather die than drink that nasty medicine."

At these words, the door flew open and four ink-black rabbits entered the room, carrying a little coffin on their shoulders.

"What do you want with me?" yelled Pinocchio, sitting bolt upright in fear.

"We've come to take you away," replied the largest rabbit.

"To take me away? But I'm not dead yet!"

"Not yet, no. But you have only a few minutes left to live, since you've refused to drink the medicine that would have cured your fever!"

"Oh Fairy, oh Fairy," the puppet began to howl, "give me that glass at once. And hurry up, for pity's sake, for I don't want to die – no, I don't want to die!"

He seized the glass in both hands and emptied it in a single swallow.

"Well then!" said the rabbits. "We made the trip for nothing this time."

And they lifted the little coffin back onto their shoulders and left the room, grousing and grumbling under their breath.

Indeed a few minutes later, Pinocchio hopped out of bed, perfectly healthy. Wooden puppets, you see, have the advantage of falling ill only rarely and of then healing quite quickly.

Seeing him running and romping around the room as spry and jolly as a young buck, the Fairy said, "So my medicine really made you feel better?"

"More than that! It brought me back to life!"

"In that case why did you make such a fuss about drinking it?"

"Because that's what all kids do! We're more afraid of taking medicine than of being sick."

"Shame on you! Children should know that the right medicine at the right time can save them from a serious illness and maybe even from death."

"Well, next time I won't make such a fuss! I'll remember those black rabbits, with that coffin on their shoulders – and then I'll grab the glass at once and drink!"

"Now come sit over here by me and tell me how it happened that you found yourself in the clutches of murderers."

"It happened because Fire-Eater, the puppet master, gave me five gold coins and said to me, 'Here, take these to your daddy,' but on the way I ran into the Fox and the Cat, two very nice fellows who said, 'Would you like these coins to become a thousand or two thousand? Come with us and we'll take you to the Field of Miracles,' and I said, 'Let's go,' and they said, 'Let's stop here at the Red Crayfish Inn, and after midnight we'll set out again,' and then when I woke up they weren't around because they had already left. So I began walking in the middle of the night, which was so dark I couldn't believe it, which is why I ran into two murderers in coal sacks who said, 'Out with your money,' and I said, 'I don't have any,' because I had hidden the gold coins in my mouth, and then one of the murderers tried to stick his hand in my mouth, so I bit it right off and spat it out, but instead of a hand it was a cat's paw. And the murderers ran after me, and I ran and ran and ran, until they caught me and strung me up by my neck from a tree in these woods, saying, 'Tomorrow we'll come back, and then you'll be dead and your mouth will be open, so we can get the gold coins you've hidden under your tongue.'"

"And where have you put the four coins now?"

"I lost them!" replied Pinocchio. But he was telling a lie – he had the coins in his pocket. As soon as he told the lie, his nose, which was already long, suddenly grew two inches longer.

"And where did you lose them?"

"In the woods, nearby."

At this second lie, his nose continued growing.

"If you lost them nearby in the woods," said the Fairy, "we'll look for them and find them, because anything that's lost nearby in the woods is always found again."

"Ah, now that I think of it," replied the puppet, getting himself in deeper, "I didn't lose the four coins, I accidentally swallowed them as I was drinking your medicine."

At this third lie, his nose grew to such an extraordinary length that poor Pinocchio could no longer even turn his head. If he turned in one direction, he banged his nose against the bed or into the windowpanes; if he turned in the other, he banged it against the wall or into the door; if he lifted his head a little, he ran the risk of poking the Fairy in the eye.

And the Fairy looked at him and laughed.

"Why are you laughing?" asked the puppet, thoroughly confounded and worried about this nose of his that was growing by leaps and bounds.

"I'm laughing at the lie you told."

"But how did you know I told a lie?"

"Lies, my boy, are immediately recognizable, for there are two kinds: lies that have short legs and lies that have long noses. Yours happen to be the long-nosed variety."

Pinocchio, wanting to hide his face in shame, tried to run from the room – but he couldn't. His nose was so long that it wouldn't fit through the doorway.

Chapter 18

As you might imagine, the Fairy let the puppet weep and wail for a good half hour about that nose of his that could no longer fit through the doorway. She did it to teach him a hard lesson, so that he might break the ugly habit of telling lies, which is the worst vice a child can have. But seeing him so transfigured, his eyes bulging out of their sockets in true despair, she was soon moved to pity, and then she clapped her hands together. At that signal a thousand woodpeckers flew through the window into the room. Every one of them perched on Pinocchio's nose, and they began pecking at it so vigorously that in a few minutes that enormous, whopping nose was restored to its natural size.

"You're such a nice Fairy," said the puppet, drying his eyes, "and I love you so much!"

"I love you, too," replied the Fairy, "and if you wish to stay with me, you can be my little brother and I your good little sister."

"I'd love to stay – but what about my poor daddy?"

"I've thought of everything. Your daddy has already been notified, and he'll be here before dark."

"Really?" shouted Pinocchio, jumping for joy. "In that case, Fairy, if it's OK with you, I'd like to go and meet him! I can't wait to give that poor old man a kiss – he's suffered so much on my account!"

"Go ahead, but be careful not to get lost. Stay on the forest path and I'm sure you'll meet him."

Pinocchio left, and as soon as he entered the forest he started running like a deer. But at a certain point, very near the Big Oak, he stopped when he thought he heard something in the bushes. Can you guess who he saw step out onto the road? The Fox and the Cat – the two travelling companions with whom he had dined at the Red Crayfish Inn.

"Here is our dear Pinocchio!" shouted the Fox, hugging and kissing him. "What are you doing here?"

"It's a long story," replied the puppet, "and I'll tell you the whole thing when I have time. But you should know that the other night, when you left me alone at the inn, I ran into some murderers on the road."

"Murderers! Oh, my poor friend! And what did they want?"

"They wanted to steal my gold coins."

"Those villains!" said the Fox.

"Those wicked villains!" repeated the Cat.

"But I started running," continued the puppet, "and they were right behind me, until they caught me and hung me from a branch of that oak."

And Pinocchio pointed to the Big Oak, a few steps away.

"Can you imagine anything worse?" said the Fox. "What a world we're condemned to live in! Where will gentlemen such as ourselves find refuge?"

As they were talking, Pinocchio noticed that the Cat's front right leg was injured – in fact, the whole paw was missing, claws and all. So he asked, "What have you done with your paw?"

The Cat tried to say something but became confused. The Fox quickly said, "My friend is too modest, that's why he's not answering. I'll answer for him. You should know that an hour ago, on this path, we encountered an old wolf who was nearly fainting with hunger – he asked us for a handout. We didn't have so much as a fishbone to give him, but what did my kindhearted friend do? He bit off one of his front paws and tossed it to the poor beast, so he would have something to eat."

As he said this, the Fox dabbed at a tear.

Pinocchio, moved too, approached the Cat and whispered in his ear, "If all cats were like you, how lucky mice would be!"

"And so, what are you doing in these parts?" the Fox asked the puppet.

"I'm waiting for my daddy, who should be coming by any minute."

"And your gold coins?"

"They're still in my pocket, except the one I spent at the Red Crayfish Inn."

"Just think, instead of four gold pieces, you could have a thousand or two thousand by tomorrow! Why don't you take my advice? Why don't you go plant them in the Field of Miracles?"

"I can't today – I'll go some other day."

"Some other day will be too late!" said the Fox.

"Why?"

"Because a rich man bought that field, and starting tomorrow no one will be allowed to plant money there."

"How far is the Field of Miracles from here?"

"Just two kilometres. Will you come with us? You could be there in half an hour, plant your four coins right away, collect two thousand after a few minutes, and be home by evening with your pockets stuffed. Will you come with us?"

Pinocchio hesitated a little before answering, as he thought of the good Fairy, of old Geppetto, and of the Talking Cricket's warnings. But in the end he did what all children with thick skulls and hard hearts do: in the end, that is, with a little shake of his head, he said to the Fox and the Cat, "Let's go then – I'm coming with you."

And so they went.

After walking half the day, they came to a city called Chumptrap. Entering the city, Pinocchio saw that the streets were full of mangy dogs yawning from hunger, fleeced sheep shivering from cold, hens with no combs or wattles begging for kernels of corn, large butterflies who could no longer fly because they had sold their beautiful wings, tailless peacocks who were ashamed to be seen, and pheasants who toddled quietly about, mourning their glittering gold-and-silver feathers, now lost for ever.

From time to time there passed, through that throng of beggars and shamefaced poor, opulent carriages containing Foxes, or thieving Magpies, or nasty Birds of Prey.

"So this Field of Miracles – where is it?" Pinocchio asked.

"It's just ahead."

Before too long, having traversed the city and passed beyond its walls, they stopped at a lonely field, one that looked more or less like every other field.

"Here we are," said the Fox to the puppet. "Now bend down to the ground, dig a little hole in the field with your hands, and put your gold coins in it."

Pinocchio obeyed. He dug the hole, he put his four remaining gold coins inside, and he covered the hole back up with dirt.

"Now then," said the Fox, "go over there to that canal, get a bucketful of water, and pour it on the spot where you've planted the coins."

Pinocchio went to the canal, and since he didn't have a bucket he took off one of his old shoes, filled it with water, and poured it on the dirt that covered the coins. Then he asked, "Anything else to do?"

"Nothing else," replied the Fox. "Now we can go. Come back in about twenty minutes and you'll find a sapling already pushing through the ground, its branches all loaded with coins."

The poor puppet, overwhelmed with happiness, thanked the Fox and the Cat a thousand times and promised them a magnificent gift.

"We want no gifts," replied those two ne'er-do-wells. "For us, it's enough that we've taught you how to get rich without having to work hard: that makes us happy as clams." With those words they waved goodbye to Pinocchio, wished him a good harvest, and went off to attend to their affairs.

Chapter 19

Back in Chumptrap, the puppet counted the minutes one by one, and when he thought it must be time, he headed down the road that led to the Field of Miracles.

His steps were quick and his heart was pounding – *tick, tock, tick, tock* – like a grandfather clock that's running too fast. And as he walked he was thinking to himself, "What if, instead of a thousand coins on the branches, I found two thousand? And what if, instead of two thousand, I found five thousand? Or instead of five thousand – a hundred thousand? Oh, what a fine gentlemen I'd be then! I'd like a big palace, a thousand wooden ponies in a thousand stalls to play with, a cellar of liqueurs and cordials, and shelves full of candied fruit, cakes, dessert breads, almond cookies, and wafers topped with whipped cream."

As he approached the field, full of such fancies, he paused to see if by chance he could make out any trees with coins on their branches. He couldn't see any yet. He walked another hundred steps – still nothing. He entered the field, and he went right up to the little hole where he had buried his gold pieces: nothing. He began to worry, and forgetting the rules of etiquette he pulled his hand from his pocket and gave his head a good long scratch.

Just then a burst of laughter shrilled in his ears, and he turned to see a large parrot sitting in a tree and grooming his few remaining feathers with his beak.

"Why are you laughing?" asked Pinocchio in a fit of temper.

"I'm laughing because I tickled myself under my wings as I was grooming my feathers."

The puppet said nothing. He went to the canal, filled his old shoe with water again, and proceeded to pour it over the dirt where he had buried his gold coins.

Just then another burst of laughter, even more obnoxious than the first, disturbed the quiet solitude of that field.

"For goodness' sake," shouted Pinocchio angrily, "what are you laughing at now, rude Parrot?"

"I'm laughing at dodos who believe every silly little thing and let themselves be tricked by those who are cleverer than they are."

"Are you by any chance talking about me?"

"Yes, I'm talking about you, poor Pinocchio – you who are so green as to believe money can be planted and harvested in fields, like beans or pumpkins. I too believed it once, and I'm still paying the price. I've come to realize (but too late!) that the only honest way to make a little money is by working with your own hands or thinking with your own head."

"I don't understand," said the puppet, already beginning to tremble with fear.

"Fine! I'll spell it out," continued the Parrot. "You see, while you were in the city, the Fox and the Cat came back to this field. They took the buried gold coins and then ran like the wind. They'll be hard to catch now!"

Pinocchio's jaw dropped. Not wanting to believe the Parrot's words, he started clawing at the dirt he had just watered. He dug and he dug and he dug, making a hole so deep you could have stood a haystack in it – but the coins were no longer there.

In desperation, he raced back to the city and made a beeline for the courthouse, to denounce to the judge those two ne'er-do-wells who had robbed him.

The judge was an ape of the Gorilla persuasion, a great big old ape, distinguished by his advanced age, by his white beard, and especially by his gold spectacles, which had no lenses, and which he had to wear at all times on account of his runny eyes, which had troubled him for years.

Pinocchio, in the judge's presence, described down to the smallest detail the wicked fraud of which he had been the victim, giving the first and last names and a description of the ne'er-do-wells, and ending by demanding justice.

The judge listened to him with great compassion, thoroughly engaged by his story. He was touched; he was moved. And when the puppet had nothing left to say, the judge reached for his bell and began waving it vigorously.

As it rang, two mastiff dogs rushed in, dressed as gendarmes.

Pointing to Pinocchio, the judge said to them, "That poor devil has been robbed of four gold coins – therefore seize him, and put him in jail at once."

The puppet, hearing this punishment befall him out of the blue, was flabbergasted and tried to protest. But the gendarmes, to avoid any pointless delays, stopped his mouth and led him off to the clink.

And there he remained for four months: four long, long months. And he would have

remained there even longer were it not for a very fortunate turn of events. You see, the young emperor who ruled the city of Chumptrap, having won a great victory over his enemies, ordered lavish public celebrations, with lights and fireworks, horse races and bicycle races – and as a sign of his great joy he even decided that the prison doors should be thrown open and all the ne'er-do-wells set free.

"If the others are getting out of prison, I want out, too," Pinocchio said to the jailer.

"Not you," said the jailer, "because you're not a ne'er-do-well."

"I beg your pardon," replied Pinocchio, "but I am so!"

"In that case, you're absolutely right," said the jailer. And doffing his cap respectfully and saying goodbye, he unlocked the door and allowed Pinocchio to go free.

Chapter 20

Imagine Pinocchio's happiness when he found himself free. Without a second thought, he quickly left the city and went back down the road that led to the Fairy's little house. On account of the drizzly weather, the whole road had turned into a bog, and with every step Pinocchio sank down to his knees. But he didn't give up. Desperately wishing to see his daddy and his Little Sister with Sky-Blue Hair, he ran in leaps and bounds like a greyhound, and as he ran the mud spattered him up to his cap. All the while he was saying to himself, "So many bad things have happened to me – and I deserved them! Because I'm a stubborn, obstinate puppet, and I always do as I please, paying no attention to those who love me, whose judgement is a thousand times better than mine! But from now on, I resolve to change my life and to become a well-behaved, obedient boy – because by now I've seen firsthand that children, if they're disobedient, always lose out and never do anything right. I wonder if my daddy has waited for me? Will I find him at the Fairy's house? Poor man, it's been so long since I've seen him, I'm dying to shower him with hugs and kisses! And will the Fairy forgive my bad behaviour? And to think she had treated me so kindly and so lovingly – and to think that it's thanks to her I'm still alive! Has there ever been a boy as ungrateful and as heartless as I am?"

He was still talking to himself like that when he suddenly came to a stop, frightened, and took four steps backwards.

What do you think he saw?

He saw, stretched across the road, a large Serpent: its skin was green, its eyes were fire, and its pointy tail was smoking like a chimney.

You can't imagine the puppet's fear. He ran more than half a kilometre away before sitting down on a little pile of stones to wait for the Serpent to go on its merry way and leave the road clear.

He waited an hour, two hours, three hours: but the Serpent was still there, and even from a distance he could see the flame in its eyes and the column of smoke rising from the tip of its tail.

Finally Pinocchio, screwing up his courage, approached to within a few steps of the Serpent, and in a sweet, wheedling voice said, "Excuse me, Mr Serpent, could you do me the favour of moving a little to one side, so that I might pass?"

He might as well have spoken to a wall. The Serpent didn't budge.

Pinocchio tried again, in the same voice: "You see, Mr Serpent, I'm going home, where my daddy is waiting for me, and it's been so long since I've seen him! Might you allow me, then, to continue on my way?"

He waited for some sign of a response to his question, but no response came. Indeed the Serpent, who up to that point had seemed full of vim and vigour, became motionless and almost rigid. His eyes closed and his tail stopped smoking.

"Could it really be dead?" said Pinocchio, rubbing his hands with glee. Without wasting a moment, he started to step across the Serpent to the far side of the road. But he had barely lifted his leg when the Serpent popped up like a spring, and the puppet, shrinking back in fear, stumbled and fell to the ground.

And he happened to fall so awkwardly that he wound up with his head stuck in the mud and his legs sticking up in the air.

At the sight of that puppet, with his head planted and his legs thrashing with incredible speed, the Serpent was overcome by a fit of laughter – he laughed and he laughed and he laughed, until the strain of laughing too hard caused a vein to burst in his chest. And then he really was dead.

So Pinocchio started running again, hoping to reach the Fairy's house before dark. But along the way, no longer able to bear the terrible pangs of hunger, he jumped into a field with the intention of picking a few bunches of muscadine grapes. If only he had never done that!

No sooner had he reached the vines when – *crack* – his legs were suddenly clamped between two very sharp pieces of metal, which made him see stars.

The poor puppet had been caught in a trap some farmers had laid for the big weasels that plagued every henhouse in the area.

Chapter 21

Pinocchio, as you can imagine, began to weep and wail and plead. But all his cries were for naught, as there were no houses in sight and not a living soul on the road.

Night fell.

Partly because of the agony of the trap that was cutting into his shins, and partly because of his fear at finding himself alone in the dark in the middle of those fields, the puppet was on the verge of fainting. Just then he saw a firefly flit over his head, so he called to her and said, "Oh, little Firefly, would you be so kind as to save me from this torture?"

"Poor child!" replied the Firefly, pausing, moved to pity by the sight of him. "How on earth did your legs end up in that sharp trap?"

"I came into the field to pick two bunches of these muscadine grapes, and—"

"But were the grapes yours?"

"No."

"Well, who taught you to take other people's belongings?"

"I was hungry."

"Hunger, my boy, is not a good reason for taking things that don't belong to us."

"It's true, it's true," shouted Pinocchio, crying, "and I'll never do it again."

At this point the conversation was interrupted by the faint noise of footsteps approaching. It was the owner of the field, coming on tiptoe to see if any of those weasels who had been eating his chickens at night had been caught in his trap.

Great was his astonishment when, pulling a lantern out from beneath his overcoat, he saw that instead of a weasel, he had caught a boy.

"Ah, little thief!" said the furious farmer. "So you're the one who makes off with my chickens!"

"Not me, not me!" shouted Pinocchio, sobbing. "I only came into the field to take a few grapes!"

"Anyone who can steal grapes is perfectly capable of stealing chickens, too. Leave it to me, I'll teach you a lesson you won't soon forget."

Opening the trap, he grabbed the puppet by the scruff of his neck and carried him home the way you'd carry a suckling lamb.

When the farmer reached the courtyard in front of his house, he threw Pinocchio on the ground and with a foot on his neck held him there and said, "It's late now and I want to go to bed. We'll settle our accounts tomorrow. Meanwhile, since my watchdog died today, you'll take his post at once. You'll be my watchdog."

With those words, he slipped a large brass-spiked collar over Pinocchio's head and tightened it around his neck so it wouldn't come off. Attached to the collar was a long iron chain – and the chain was fastened to the wall.

"If it should rain tonight," the farmer said, "you can go lie down in that wooden doghouse – the straw my poor dog slept on these past four years is still there. And remember to keep an ear out for thieves, and if any should come around, be sure to bark."

After this warning, the farmer went inside and bolted the door. And poor Pinocchio was left crouching in the courtyard, more dead than alive from cold, from hunger, and from fear. Every now and then he angrily tugged at his collar, which was tight on his throat, and said through his tears, "It serves me right! Alas, it serves me right! I acted like an idler and a vagabond. I listened to bad advice, and so now bad luck follows me wherever I go. If only I had been a good little boy, like so many others; if only I had been willing to study and work; if only I had stayed home with my poor daddy, then I wouldn't find myself here, in the middle of this field, serving as a watchdog outside a farmer's house. Oh, if I could only start over! But it's too late now, and I must be patient!"

After this little outburst, which was truly from the heart, he crawled into the doghouse and fell asleep.

Chapter 22

He had been sound asleep for more than two hours when, around midnight, he was awoken by the whispers and murmurs of strange little voices, which seemed to come from the courtyard. He poked his nose out of the doghouse and saw four dark-furred creatures holding council. They looked a bit like cats, but they weren't cats: they were weasels, carnivorous little beasts with a strong weakness for eggs and young hens. One of these weasels, turning away from his companions, came over to the doghouse door and said, "Good evening, Tiresias."

"My name is not Tiresias," replied the puppet.

"Who are you then?"

"I am Pinocchio."

"And what are you doing in there?"

"I'm serving as a watchdog."

"But where's Tiresias? Where's the old dog who lived in this doghouse?"

"He died this morning."

"Died? Poor beast! He was such a good dog! But judging by the looks of you, I'd say you're a friendly dog, too."

"I beg your pardon – I'm not a dog!"

"Then what are you?"

"I'm a puppet."

"And you're serving as a watchdog?"

"Unfortunately, as punishment!"

"OK then, I'll offer you the same terms I had with the late Tiresias – you'll be pleased."

"And what might these terms be?"

"We'll come once a week, as in the past, and we'll take eight hens. Of these eight, seven will be for us to eat, and one will be for you – on the condition, of course, that you pretend to be sleeping and never get the urge to bark and wake the farmer."

"Did Tiresias really do that?" Pinocchio asked.

"He did, which is why we always got along just fine. So sleep tight, and rest assured that before we go we'll leave a nice plucked hen outside your doghouse for your morning

breakfast. Do we understand each other?"

"All too well!" replied Pinocchio, nodding his head in an almost threatening way, as if to say: *This isn't over yet!*

The four weasels, now confident in their plan, went straight to the henhouse, which indeed was right there beside the doghouse. With a flurry of claws and teeth, they unlocked the little wooden door that blocked the entrance and they slipped inside, one by one. The last weasel was barely in when they all heard the little door slam violently shut behind them.

It was Pinocchio who had shut it. And not content with merely closing the little door, he propped a large rock against it, for extra security.

And then he began to bark – and he barked just like a real watchdog, like this: *woof, woof, woof, woof.*

Hearing the barks, the farmer jumped out of bed, grabbed his rifle, and stuck his head out the window.

"What's going on?" he asked.

"The thieves are here!" replied Pinocchio.

"Where?"

"In the henhouse."

"I'll be right down."

And quicker than you could say "amen" the farmer came down. He rushed into the henhouse, and after grabbing the four weasels and sticking them in a sack, he said in a genuinely happy voice, "Finally you've fallen into my hands! I could punish you, but I'm not so mean-spirited! I'll content myself, rather, with taking you tomorrow to the innkeeper of the neighboring town, who'll skin you and cook you like hares, in a soursweet sauce. It's an honour you don't deserve, but generous men, like me, can overlook such trifles!"

Then he went over to Pinocchio and gave him a big hug, and eventually he got around to asking him, "How did you manage to discover the plot of these four little thieves? And to think that Tiresias, my faithful Tiresias, never caught on at all!"

The puppet, now, could have recounted everything he knew. He could, in other words, have told about the shameful pact that existed between the dog and the weasels.

But remembering that the dog was dead, he immediately thought: "What good does it do to accuse the dead? The dead are dead, and the best thing to do is to leave them in peace!"

"When the weasels came into the courtyard, were you awake or asleep?" the farmer now asked him.

"I was asleep," replied Pinocchio, "but the weasels woke me up with their chattering, and one of them came up to the doghouse to tell me: 'If you promise not to bark and not to wake your master, we'll give you a nice plucked chicken!' Can you imagine? To have the gall to propose something like that to me! You see, I may be a puppet, and I may have every fault under the sun, but I would never get mixed up with dishonest folk!"

"Good boy!" shouted the farmer, slapping him on the back. "Such sentiments do you honour. And to show you how pleased I am, I'm setting you free right now so you can go home."

And he took the dog collar off.

Chapter 23

As soon as the hard, humiliating weight of that collar was lifted from his neck, Pinocchio began dashing across the fields, and he didn't stop for single moment until he reached the main road that he knew should lead back to the Fairy's little house.

Once on the main road, he looked down the hill to the flat country below, and there, perfectly visible to the naked eye, was the forest where he had, alas, encountered the Fox and the Cat. He could see, rising above the other trees, the top of the Big Oak, from which he had been left dangling by the neck. But he could not see, though he looked this way and that, the little house of the Beautiful Girl with Sky-Blue Hair.

Suddenly he had a dreadful premonition, and running with all the strength left in his legs he soon found himself in the clearing where the little white house had once stood. But the little white house was no longer there. In its place stood a small slab of marble on which could be read, in block letters, these painful words:

HERE LIES

THE GIRL WITH SKY-BLUE HAIR

WHO DIED OF GRIEF

AFTER BEING ABANDONED BY HER

LITTLE BROTHER PINOCCHIO

After struggling mightily to read those words, Pinocchio felt – well, I'll let you imagine how he felt. He fell forwards onto the ground, covered the gravestone with a thousand kisses, and burst into tears. He cried all through the night, and the next morning when the sun came up he was crying still, though by this point he had no tears left in his eyes. His cries and laments were so heartrending and piercing that all of the surrounding hills kept repeating their echo.

And as he cried, he said, "Oh, little Fairy, why did you die? Why couldn't I have died instead, I who am so wicked, while you were so good? And where in the world is my daddy? Oh, little Fairy, please tell me you're not really dead! If you truly love your little brother, come back to life – come back like you were before! Doesn't it bother you to see me alone, abandoned by everyone? If the murderers come, they'll hang me again

from that branch – and then I'll die for ever. What do you want me to do, all alone in this world? Now that I've lost you and my daddy, who will feed me? Where will I sleep at night? Who'll make me a new jacket? Oh, it would be better, a hundred times better, if I died, too! Yes, I want to die! Boo-hoo-hoo!"

Despairing in this fashion, he made as if to tear out his hair. But since his hair was wooden, he didn't even have the satisfaction of sticking his fingers into it.

Just then a great Pigeon, hovering above him on extended wings, shouted down from a great height, "Tell me, child, what are you doing down there?"

"Can't you see? I'm crying!" Pinocchio said, looking up at that voice and rubbing his eyes with his coat sleeve.

"Say," added the Pigeon, "you wouldn't by any chance happen to know someone – a puppet – named Pinocchio?"

"Pinocchio? Did you say Pinocchio?" repeated the puppet, jumping to his feet. "I'm Pinocchio!"

Hearing this, the Pigeon swooped down and landed on the ground. He was larger than a turkey.

"Then you must know Geppetto, too!"

"Know him! He's my poor daddy! Did he by any chance tell you about me? Can you take me to him? Is he still alive? Answer me, please: Is he still alive?"

"I left him three days ago on the seashore."

"What was he doing?"

"He was building himself a rowboat, to cross the ocean in. For more than four months that poor man has been roaming the world looking for you. And having failed to find you, he has now gotten the notion to look for you in the distant lands of the New World."

"How far is it from here to the shore?" Pinocchio asked with breathless worry.

"More than a thousand kilometres."

"A thousand kilometres? Oh, dear Pigeon, how happy I'd be if I had your wings!"

"If you wish to go, I'll take you myself."

"How?"

"You can ride on my back. Are you heavy?"

"Heavy? Not at all! I'm light as a feather."

And so, without another word, Pinocchio leapt onto the Pigeon's back. Straddling the bird like a horse, he shouted happily, "Gallop, gallop, little horsey – I have to get there soon!"

The Pigeon took flight and soon was soaring so high that they almost touched the clouds.

Having reached that extraordinary height, the puppet turned, out of curiosity, and looked down, which left him so scared and dizzy that he looped his arms ever so tightly around the neck of his feathered mount, to keep from falling off.

They flew all day. Towards evening, the Pigeon said, "I'm very thirsty!"

"And I'm very hungry," added Pinocchio.

"Let's stop for a few minutes at this pigeon coop, then resume our journey again, so we can reach the seashore by tomorrow morning."

In the deserted pigeon coop they found only a bowl full of water and a basket heaped with vetch peas.

The puppet had never, in his whole life, been able to stand vetch peas. He said they nauseated him, turned his stomach. But that evening he ate them until he nearly burst, and when he had almost finished, he turned to the Pigeon and said, "I'd never have believed that vetch peas could taste so good!"

"You have to realize, my boy," replied the Pigeon, "that when hunger is real and there's nothing else to eat, even vetch peas become delicious! Hunger's neither picky nor greedy."

They wolfed down their snack and were on their way again. The next morning they reached the seashore.

The Pigeon set Pinocchio down, and not wishing to be bothered even with thanks for his good deed, flew off at once and disappeared.

The beach was crowded with people looking out to sea, shouting and gesticulating.

"What happened?" Pinocchio asked a little old woman.

"What happened is that some poor father who has lost his son has decided to row a boat across the sea to look for him on the other side. But the sea today is very rough and his boat is about to go under."

"Where is the boat?"

"Over there, where I'm pointing," said the old woman, aiming her finger at a small boat that looked, from this distance, like a walnut shell with an itty-bitty man in it.

After gazing carefully in that direction, Pinocchio let out a piercing shriek: "That's my daddy! That's my daddy!"

Meanwhile the boat, battered by the raging sea, now disappeared between the enormous waves, now rose upon their crests. Pinocchio, standing on a high rock, never stopped calling out to his daddy or signalling to him – with his hands and his hankie and even with his cap.

And it seemed that Geppetto, though far from shore, recognized his son, for he also took off his cap and waved it, indicating with wild gestures that he would gladly come back, but that the sea was so rough that he was unable to work his oars to get closer to shore.

Suddenly there was a terrifying wave, and the boat disappeared. Everyone waited for it to rise up again, but no trace of it remained.

"Poor man," said the fishermen who were gathered there on the shore. And muttering a prayer beneath their breath, they turned to go back to their homes.

Just then they heard a desperate cry, and looking back they saw a little boy throwing himself from a high rock into the sea, shouting, "I will save my daddy!"

Since he was made entirely of wood, Pinocchio floated easily and could swim like a fish. People watched him swim, now disappearing beneath the surface, carried by the strength of the current, and now reappearing with an arm or a leg, a great distance from land. Finally they lost sight of him completely.

"Poor boy," said the fishermen who were gathered there on the shore. And muttering a prayer beneath their breath, they went back to their homes.

Chapter 24

Pinocchio, driven by the hope of arriving in time to help his poor daddy, swam all through the night. And what a horrible night it was! It poured, it hailed, it thundered menacingly, and the flashes of lightning sometimes made it bright as day.

Near dawn, he spied a long strip of land nearby. It was an island in the middle of the sea.

He tried his best to reach its shore – but in vain. The waves, racing and tumbling over each other, tossed him about as if he were a twig or a piece of straw. At last, and fortunately for him, there came a wave so mighty and ferocious that it hurled him bodily onto the sandy beach.

He hit the ground so hard that all his ribs and joints cracked, but he quickly consoled himself by saying, "Once again I've made a narrow escape!"

Meanwhile the sky gradually cleared, the sun came out in all its glory, and the sea became as smooth and gentle as oil.

After laying his clothes out to dry in the sun, the puppet began to look this way and that, hoping he might spot, out on that vast expanse of water, a little rowboat with a tiny man inside. But no matter how hard he looked, he saw nothing before him but the sky, the sea, and a few sails, so far away they looked like flies.

"I wish I at least knew what this island is called!" he said. "I wish I at least knew if this island was inhabited by well-mannered people – I mean, people who aren't in the habit of hanging children from tree branches! But just who can I ask? Who – if nobody's here?"

This thought of finding himself all alone, all alone in that big uninhabited land, put him in such a sad mood that he was on the verge of tears. At that moment, a short distance from the shore, he saw an enormous fish swimming by, going quietly about his business, with his whole head above the water.

Not knowing the fish's name, the puppet called loudly to him: "Hey, Mr Fish, could I have a word with you?"

"Two if you like," replied the fish, who was a dolphin – and one of the nicest ones in all the seas of the world.

"Would you be so kind as to tell me if there are villages on this island where one might get something to eat, without the danger of getting eaten?"

"There certainly are," replied the Dolphin. "Indeed, you'll find one not far from here."

"Which way should I go to get there?"

"Just go straight down that path there, to your left, and follow your nose. You can't miss it."

"I have one more question. Since you roam the sea all day and all night, I wonder if by any chance you've come across a little rowboat with my daddy in it?"

"And who might your daddy be?"

"He's the best daddy in the world, just as I'm the worst of sons."

"With that storm we had last night," replied the Dolphin, "the little rowboat must have sunk."

"And my daddy?"

"By now he has probably been swallowed by the terrible Shark, who came to our waters several days ago to spread death and woe."

"This Shark, is he very big?" asked Pinocchio, already trembling with fear.

"Is he big!" replied the Dolphin. "To give you an idea, I'll tell you that he's bigger than a five-storey house, with a mouth so wide and deep that an entire railway train could easily pass through it with its locomotive steaming."

"Oh dear!" cried the frightened puppet. Hastily putting his clothes back on, he turned to the Dolphin and said, "Farewell, Mr Fish – please excuse the bother, and a thousand thanks for your kindness."

With these words, he made straight for the path and began walking quickly down it – so quickly he almost seemed to be running. And at the slightest noise, he would turn around suddenly, afraid he was being followed by that terrible Shark that was big as a five-storey house and had a railway train in his mouth.

After walking more than half an hour, he came to a small village called Busy-Bee Village. The streets swarmed with people going this way and that about their business: all were working, all had something to do. You couldn't have found a loafer or a layabout even if you looked with a magnifying glass.

"I can see," thought that lazybones Pinocchio at once, "that this is not my kind of village. I wasn't born to work!"

Meanwhile his hunger was gnawing at him because he hadn't eaten a thing for more than twenty-four hours – not even a bowl of vetch peas.

What to do?

He saw only two ways to break his fast: either ask for a little work, or beg for a penny or a bite of bread.

He was ashamed to beg, because his father had always preached that only the old and the sick have a right to beg. The real poor in this world, the ones who deserve assistance and compassion, are the ones who because of age or illness are unable to support themselves with the labour of their own hands. All the rest have an obligation to work – and if they choose not to and go hungry, then too bad for them.

Just then a sweaty, breathless man came slogging down the road, pulling two brimming carts of coal all by himself, with great effort.

Judging him to be a kind man by the look of his face, Pinocchio approached, eyes cast down with shame, and said meekly, "Would you be so kind as to give me a penny, for I feel I'm dying of hunger?"

"I won't give you just one penny," replied the coalman, "I'll give you four, if you'll help me pull these two carts of coal to my house."

"I'm astonished!" replied the puppet, as if offended. "For your information, I've never served as a donkey – I've never pulled a cart!"

"Good for you!" replied the coalman. "In that case, my boy, if you're really dying of hunger, eat two big slices of your pride, and take care not to get indigestion."

After a few minutes, a bricklayer passed by, carrying a hod of mortar on his shoulder.

"Would you give a penny, kind sir, to a poor boy who is yawning from hunger?"

"Gladly," replied the mason. "Help me carry this mortar and instead of one penny I'll give you five."

"But mortar is heavy," replied Pinocchio, "and I don't want to work hard."

"If you don't want to work hard, my boy, then have fun yawning – I hope it makes you happy."

In less than half an hour, another twenty people passed, and Pinocchio begged alms from all of them, but all replied: "Aren't you ashamed? Instead of being an idler on the street, why don't you look for some work instead, and learn to earn your bread!"

At last there came a good little woman carrying two jugs of water.

"Good woman, would you allow me to take a sip of water from your jug?" said Pinocchio, who was burning with thirst.

"Go ahead and drink, my boy!" said the little woman, setting down the two jugs.

After drinking like a sponge, Pinocchio mumbled, as he wiped his mouth, "I've quenched my thirst! If only I could satisfy my hunger so easily!"

The good little woman, hearing these words, added at once: "If you help me carry one of these jugs home, I'll give you a nice piece of bread."

Pinocchio looked at the jug but didn't say either yes or no.

"And along with the bread I'll give you a nice plate of cauliflower dressed with oil and vinegar."

Pinocchio took another look at the jug, but didn't say either yes or no.

"And after the cauliflower, I'll give you a nice bonbon with a sweet rosewater filling."

The temptation of this final delicacy was too much for Pinocchio to resist, so he made up his mind and said, "All right! I'll carry the jug to your house!"

The jug was too heavy for the puppet to carry in his arms, and so he resigned himself to carrying it on top of his head.

When they reached her house, the good little woman sat Pinocchio down at a little table that was already set, and she placed before him the bread, the dressed cauliflower, and the bonbon.

Pinocchio didn't eat – he devoured. His stomach was like an apartment that had been vacant for five months.

When his ferocious pangs of hunger began gradually to subside, he lifted his head to thank his benefactress. But no sooner did he see her face than he let out a prolonged *ohhh!* of amazement, and sat there enchanted, his eyes wide, his fork in midair, his mouth full of bread and cauliflower.

"What are you so amazed about?" the good woman said, laughing.

"It's just," stammered Pinocchio, "it's just . . . it's just . . . that you look like . . . you remind me . . . yes, yes, yes, the same voice . . . the same eyes . . . the same hair . . . yes, yes, yes . . . you have sky-blue hair, too – like her! My little Fairy! Oh, my little Fairy! Tell me it's you, really you! Don't make me cry any more! If you only knew! I've cried so much, I've suffered so much!"

As he spoke these words, sobbing copiously, Pinocchio dropped down to the floor and threw his arms around the knees of that mysterious little woman.

Chapter 25

At first, the good little woman was about to say she was not the little Fairy with Sky-Blue Hair. But realizing she had been found out and not wanting to pretend any longer, she decided to admit the truth, saying to Pinocchio, "You scamp of a puppet! How did you know it was me?"

"It was my great love for you, that's what told me."

"You remember, do you? You left me a girl, and now you find me a woman – so grown up I could almost be your mother."

"And that gladdens my heart, because now, instead of my sister, I'll call you my mother. For so long I have been yearning to have a mother, like other children! But how did you manage to grow up so fast?"

"It's a secret."

"Teach me how – I'd like to grow up a little, too. Don't you see? I'm about as tall as a piece of cheese."

"But you can't grow," replied the Fairy.

"Why not?"

"Because puppets never grow. They're born as puppets, they live as puppets, and they die as puppets."

"Oh, I'm sick of always being just a puppet!" shouted Pinocchio, smacking himself on the forehead. "It's about time I grew up too and became a man."

"And you will, if you can earn it."

"Really? How do I earn it?"

"It's the easiest thing in the world: just practise being a proper boy."

"But aren't I one already?"

"Not at all! Proper boys are obedient, and you on the other hand—"

"I never obey."

"Proper boys take pleasure in study and in work, while you—"

"While I on the other hand am always an idler and a vagabond."

"Proper boys always tell the truth—"

"And I'm always telling lies."

"Proper boys like going to school—"

"And school gives me a stomachache. But from now on I'm going to change my life."

"Promise me?"

"I promise. I want to become a proper boy, and I want to be a comfort to my daddy – where can my poor daddy be now?"

"I don't know."

"Will I ever be lucky enough to see him and hug him again?"

"I think so – indeed, I am sure of it."

On hearing these words Pinocchio was nearly beside himself with happiness, so much so that he grabbed the Fairy's hands and began fervently kissing them. Then lifting his face and looking lovingly at her, he asked, "So tell me, dear mother, it isn't true that you were dead?"

"It would seem not," replied the Fairy, smiling.

"If you only knew how miserable and choked up I was, when I read *Here Lies*—"

"I do know. That's why I've forgiven you. The sincerity of your grief showed me that you had a good heart. And with good-hearted children, even if they're a bit naughty and have some bad habits, there's always some hope – hope that they'll mend their ways, I mean. That's why I came all the way here to look for you. I'll be your mother—"

"Oh, how wonderful!" shouted Pinocchio, jumping for joy.

"—and you'll obey me and always do what I tell you to do—"

"Gladly, gladly, gladly!"

"—and tomorrow," added the Fairy, "you'll start going to school—"

Pinocchio suddenly grew slightly less cheerful.

"—and you'll choose an art or a trade of your liking—"

Pinocchio grew serious.

"What are you muttering under your breath?" asked the Fairy, in an angry tone.

"I was saying," whimpered the puppet, "that it seems, by now, a little late for me to start school."

"No sirree. Keep in mind that it's never too late to learn and to educate ourselves."

"But I don't want to do any art or any trade."

"Why not?"

"Because work seems tiring."

"Dear boy," said the Fairy, "people who talk that way almost always end up either in a prison or a poorhouse. For your information, everyone, whether they're born rich or poor, is obliged to do something – to keep busy, to work. Woe to anyone who yields to idleness! Idleness is a dreadful disease and must be treated at once, starting in childhood. If not, it will be too late by the time we grow up."

These words touched Pinocchio's heart, and he quickly lifted his head and said to the Fairy, "I'll go to school, I'll work, I'll do everything you tell me, because, well, I've grown tired of living the life of a puppet, and I want to become a boy at any cost. You promised, right?"

"I did indeed, and now it's up to you."

Chapter 26

The next day Pinocchio went to the local school.

Imagine those little scamps, seeing a puppet come to their school! They couldn't stop laughing. They played one trick after another on him: one snatched his cap, one yanked his little jacket from behind, one tried to draw a big moustache under his nose in ink, and one even tried to tie strings to his hands and feet to make him dance.

For a while, Pinocchio maintained his composure and kept his distance. But finally, feeling his patience running out, he turned to the ones who were pestering him and making sport of him the most, and he told them sternly, "Watch out, boys, I didn't come here to be the butt of your jokes. I respect others and I want to be respected."

"Bravo, dunce! You speak like a printed book!" howled the rascals, falling over with laughter. And one of them, the cheekiest of the bunch, reached out his hand intending to seize the puppet by the end of his nose.

But he wasn't quick enough: Pinocchio stuck his leg out under the table and gave him a kick on the shins.

"Ouch! What hard feet!" cried the boy, rubbing the bruise the puppet had given him.

"And what elbows – even harder than his feet!" said another, who in return for one of his rude tricks had received an elbow in the belly.

The fact is that after that kick and that elbow, Pinocchio swiftly gained the admiration and the sympathy of all the boys in school. They all took a heartfelt liking to him and began showering him with affection.

And even the teacher boasted about him, for he could see that Pinocchio was attentive, hardworking, intelligent, always the first to arrive at school and the last to get out of his seat at the end of the day.

His only fault was knocking about with too many of his schoolmates. Among them were a bunch of rogues notorious for their lack of interest in studying or doing well in school.

His teacher warned him every day, and even the good Fairy told him over and over again: "Watch out, Pinocchio! Sooner or later those naughty schoolmates of yours will end up causing you to lose all love for learning, and they might, just might, get you into some big trouble."

"Don't worry!" the puppet replied, shrugging and tapping his index finger on his forehead, as if to say: "There's a lot of good sense in here!"

Then one fine day, as he was walking to school, he happened to run into his usual flock of friends. As they approached, they said, "Have you heard the big news?"

"No."

"A shark as big as a mountain has appeared nearby in the sea."

"Really?"

"We're going to the beach to see it. You want to come, too?"

"Not me. I want to go to school."

"Who cares about school? We can go to school tomorrow. One day more or less of school – we'll still be the same old jackasses."

"But what will the teacher say?"

"The teacher can say whatever he likes. He's paid to spend his days grumbling."

"And my mother?"

"Mothers never know anything," replied those rogues.

"You know what I'll do?" Pinocchio said. "I want to see that Shark for certain reasons of my own – but I'll go and see it after school."

"Silly fool!" retorted one of the flock. "Do you think that a fish of that magnitude will hang around until it suits you? As soon as he gets bored, he'll blunder off somewhere else, and that will be that."

"How long does it take to get from here to the beach?" the puppet asked.

"We can be there and back in an hour."

"Then let's go! And the last one there's a rotten egg!"

The starting signal having thus been given, that flock of rogues began to sprint across the fields, with their books and notebooks under their arms. And Pinocchio was always in the lead; he seemed to have wings on his feet.

Every now and then he turned back to taunt his friends, who were a considerable distance behind him, and seeing them panting and gasping and covered with dust, their tongues hanging out, he laughed at them heartily. The wretch, in that moment, had no idea what frights and what terrible troubles lay in store for him!

Chapter 27

When he reached the shore, Pinocchio began scanning the sea. But he didn't see any Shark. The sea was perfectly smooth, like a giant mirror.

"The Shark – where is it?" he asked, turning to his companions.

"Maybe he went to breakfast," replied one of his companions, laughing.

"Or maybe he went back to bed for a little nap," added another, laughing even harder.

From these absurd answers and their silly cackling, Pinocchio gathered that his schoolmates had played a cruel trick on him. His feelings hurt, Pinocchio said to them in a furious voice, "Now what? What have you gained by making me believe that fib about the Shark?"

"We've gained plenty!" those rogues replied in chorus.

"Such as?"

"We've made you skip school and come with us. Aren't you ashamed of being so punctual and hardworking every day at school? Aren't you ashamed of studying as much as you do?"

"What difference does it make to you if I study?"

"It makes a big difference, because you make us look bad to the teacher."

"How?"

"Because the kids who study always make the kids who don't want to study, like us, look bad by comparison. And we don't want to look bad! We have some self-respect, too!"

"So what do I have to do to make you happy?"

"You have to be fed up, like us, with the school and the lessons and the teacher – our three great enemies."

"And what if I want to keep studying?"

"We'll never look you in the face again, and we'll make you pay the first chance we get!"

"To tell the truth, you almost make me laugh," said the puppet, shaking his head.

"Hey, Pinocchio!" shouted the biggest of the boys, walking right up to him. "You better not act like a tough guy here! You better not act so cocky! Because you might not be afraid of us, but we're not afraid of you, either! And don't forget there's one of you and seven of us."

"Seven – like the seven deadly sins," said Pinocchio, laughing.

"Did you hear that? He insulted all of us! He called us deadly sins!"

"Pinocchio, you better apologize – or else!"

"Nanny-nanny-boo-boo!" said the puppet, thumbing his nose to mock them.

"Pinocchio! You'll be sorry!"

"Nanny-nanny-boo-boo!"

"We'll beat you like a donkey!"

"Nanny-nanny-boo-boo!"

"We'll send you home with a broken nose!"

"Nanny-nanny-boo-boo!"

"You'll get the boo-boo now!" shouted the boldest of those rogues. "Here's a taste to start with, and you can save the rest for supper!"

And as he said that, he punched Pinocchio in the head.

But it was tit for tat, as the saying goes, because the puppet, as might be expected, answered at once with a counterpunch. And from then on, the battle became general and fierce.

Though Pinocchio was alone, he defended himself like a hero. He used those rock-hard wooden feet of his so well that his enemies were forced to keep a respectful distance. Wherever his feet could reach and strike, they left souvenir bruises.

At this point, the boys, vexed at being unable to match the puppet in hand-to-hand combat, thought it wise to resort to projectiles. They untied their bundles of schoolbooks and began flinging them at Pinocchio: their spelling books, their grammar books, Thouar's *Popular Tales*, Baccini's *Memoirs of a Chick*, a couple of books by a fellow named Collodi, and still others. But the puppet, who was sharp-eyed and quick-witted, always managed to duck in time, so that all the books sailed over his head and dropped into the sea.

Think of the fish! Believing that those books were something good to eat, whole schools of fish swarmed to the water's surface. But after sampling a page here and a frontispiece there, they spat them right back out, making the sort of face that seemed to say, "This stuff is not for us: we are accustomed to much better fare!"

Meanwhile, as the battle was growing fiercer and fiercer, a large Crab, who had crawled ever so slowly out of the water and onto the beach, shouted out in an ugly voice that sounded like a trombone with a cold, "Cut it out, you incorrigible rascals! These fistfights between boys and boys never end well. They always end in disaster!"

Poor Crab! He might as well have been preaching to the wind. And indeed that rogue Pinocchio turned and scowled at him, saying rudely, "Oh hush, you tiresome Crab! You'd be better off sucking on some lozenges to cure that cold of yours. Or else go to bed and try to sweat it out!"

By this time the boys, who had finished throwing all their own books, spotted the puppet's bundle of books lying nearby, and quick as a wink they snatched them up.

Among these books was one that had a thick hard cover and vellum on the spine and corners. It was called *Treatise on Arithmetic*. I'll let you imagine how heavy it was!

One of those rascals snatched up that volume and, aiming at Pinocchio's head, flung it with all his might. But instead of hitting the puppet, it struck the head of one of his companions, who turned white as a washed sheet. All he said, before collapsing onto the sand, were these words: "Oh, mother, help me – for I am dying."

At the sight of that dead-looking boy, his frightened companions took to their heels; in the blink of an eye they were out of sight.

But Pinocchio stayed behind. And though he, too, from grief and fright, was more dead than alive, nevertheless he ran to soak his handkerchief in seawater, and he began to bathe his poor schoolmate's temples. Pinocchio sobbed and despaired and called his schoolmate's name and said, "Eugenio! My poor Eugenio! Open your eyes and look at me! Why aren't you answering? I'm not the one, you know, who hurt you like this! Believe me, it wasn't me! Open your eyes, Eugenio! If you keep your eyes closed, you'll make me die, too! Oh, God! How can I go back home now? How can I dare face my good mother? What will become of me? Where will I run to? Where will I hide? Oh, how much better it would have been – a thousand times better – if I had gone to school today! Why did I listen to those schoolmates who are the bane of my life! The teacher even told me so! And my mother told me over and over: 'Beware of keeping bad company!' But I'm too stubborn, too headstrong. I always let them talk, but then I just do as I please! And I end up paying for it. And so, for as long as I've been in the world, I've never had fifteen minutes of peace. Oh, God! What will become of me, what will become of me, what will become of me!"

And Pinocchio kept crying, and bawling, and hitting himself in the head, and calling poor Eugenio by name – when he suddenly heard the muffled sound of approaching footsteps.

He turned, and there stood two policemen.

"What are you doing here, stretched out on the ground?"

"I'm helping this schoolmate of mine."

"Has he fallen ill?"

"It looks that way."

"He isn't ill!" said one of the policemen, leaning down to look closely at Eugenio. "This boy has been wounded in the temple – who wounded him?"

"Not me!" sputtered the puppet, who could barely breathe.

"If it wasn't you, then who did wound him?"

"Not me!" Pinocchio said again.

"And what was he wounded with?"

"With this book."

"And whose book might this be?"

"Mine."

"That's enough – we don't need to know anything else. Get up right now and come along with us."

"But I—"

"Come with us!"

"But I'm innocent—"

"Come with us!"

Before leaving, the policemen called out to some fishermen, who just in that moment happened to be passing by, and said to them, "We're giving you this boy who has been wounded in the head. Carry him home with you and take care of him. Tomorrow we'll come by to see him."

Then they turned back to Pinocchio, put him between them, and commanded him in soldierly voices: "Forward march! On the double! Or you'll be sorry!"

Not needing to be told twice, Pinocchio began walking down that path, which led to town. The poor devil barely knew what had hit him. He thought he must be dreaming, and what an awful dream it was! He was beside himself. He was seeing double, his legs

were wobbly, his tongue was stuck to the roof of his mouth, and he couldn't spit out a single word.

And yet, through that stupor and bewilderment, one very sharp thorn was piercing his heart: I mean the thought of having to walk, escorted by policemen, past the windows of the good Fairy's house. He would have rather died.

They reached the edge of town and were about to enter it when a rough gust of wind lifted Pinocchio's cap from his head and blew it ten paces away.

"Would you permit me," the puppet asked the policemen, "to retrieve my cap?"

"Go ahead, but be quick about it."

The puppet went and picked up his cap – but instead of putting it back on his head, he put it between his teeth and started running full tilt towards the seashore. He was fast as a bullet.

The policemen, seeing they would have a hard time catching up, sent a dog after him, a great big mastiff dog, who had won first prize in all the dog races. Pinocchio ran, and the dog ran faster. Soon people were leaning out their windows and flocking to the road, eager to see the outcome of such a furious sprint. But their curiosity went unsatisfied, because between them Pinocchio and that mastiff dog kicked up such a cloud of dust that after a few minutes nobody could see anything.

Chapter 28

During that desperate race a terrible moment came, a moment in which Pinocchio thought he was lost. You see, Wingfoot (that was the mastiff dog's name), after running and running, had almost caught him.

Let's just say that the puppet could hear, a handbreadth away, the laboured panting of that nasty beast, and he could even feel the hot blasts of his smelly breath.

As luck would have it, the beach was now close at hand and the sea just a few steps away.

As soon as he gained the beach, the puppet leapt magnificently into the air, as a bullfrog might have done, and landed with a splash in the water. Wingfoot, however, tried to stop, but his momentum carried him into the water as well. Since the poor wretch didn't know how to swim, he began flailing about with his paws to stay afloat. But the more he flailed, the more his head went under.

When his head resurfaced, the poor dog's eyes were bulging with terror and, barking, he cried, "I'm drowning! I'm drowning!"

"Drop dead!" replied Pinocchio from afar, seeing that by now he was safe from danger.

"Help me, dear Pinocchio! Save me from death!"

At that pitiful cry, the puppet (who deep down had a very good heart) was moved to compassion, and he turned to the dog and said, "If I help save you, do you promise to stop bothering and chasing me?"

"I promise! I promise! Hurry up, for heaven's sake – if you wait another half minute I'll be as good as dead."

Pinocchio hesitated a little, but then he remembered how many times his daddy had told him that a good deed is never lost, and he swam over to Wingfoot, took hold of his tail with both hands, and pulled him safe and sound onto the dry sand of the beach.

The poor dog could no longer stand. Without meaning to, he had swallowed so much salt water that he was as swollen as a balloon. The puppet, however, not wanting to take any chances, thought it wise to throw himself back into the sea. And as he swam away from shore, he shouted to his rescued friend, "Goodbye, Wingfoot! Happy travels and all my best to you and yours."

"Goodbye, Pinocchio," replied the dog. "A thousand thanks for saving me from death. You've done me a good turn, and in this world one good turn deserves another. If the occasion arises, you never know . . ."

Pinocchio kept on swimming, keeping the shore always in sight. Finally he felt he had come to a safe place, and glancing at the shore he saw, among the rocks, a sort of cave, from which was rising a very long plume of smoke.

"In that cave," Pinocchio thought to himself, "there must be a fire. So much the better! I'll go dry off and warm up – and then? And then we'll see what happens."

Having made this decision, he approached the rocks. But as he was getting ready to climb out, he felt something beneath him in the water that rose and rose and rose and lifted him into the air. He immediately tried to get free, but it was too late: to his great astonishment he found himself caught in a large fishing net, amid a swarm of fish of every size and shape who were thrashing and struggling like doomed souls.

At the same time he saw, emerging from the cave, a fisherman so ugly that he looked like a sea monster. Instead of hair, a thick bush of green grass grew atop his head, green was his skin, green his eyes, green the long, long beard that hung down to here. He looked like a big lizard standing on its hind legs.

As the fisherman pulled the net out of the sea, he shouted happily, "Blessed Providence! Once again I can stuff myself to the gills with fish!"

"Lucky for me I'm not a fish," Pinocchio thought to himself, plucking up his courage.

The fisherman carried the net loaded with fish into his cave, a dark and smoky cave in the middle of which a big skillet of oil was sizzling, giving off such a whiff of candle snuff as to take your breath away.

"Now let's see what fishes we've caught!" said the green fisherman. Thrusting into the net a hand so huge it looked like a baker's peel, he pulled out a handful of goatfish.

"Tasty, these goatfish!" he said, eyeing them and sniffing them with pleasure. After sniffing them, he tossed them into a big bucket with no water in it.

Then he repeated the same process several more times. And as he plucked the other fishes out, his mouth began to water and he said, with glee, "Tasty, these hake! Scrumptious, these mullet! Delectable, these sole! Choice, these sea bass! Cute, these anchovies with their heads on!"

As you can guess, the hake, the mullet, the sole, the sea bass, and the anchovies all went pell-mell into the bucket, to keep the goatfish company.

The last thing remaining in the net was Pinocchio.

As soon as the fisherman had plucked out Pinocchio, his big green eyes bulged with astonishment and he yelled, as though frightened, "What manner of fish is this? I don't recall ever eating this sort of fish!"

And he looked him over carefully again, and after scrutinizing him from every angle, he declared, "I know – this must be a sea slug."

Mortified at being mistaken for a slug, Pinocchio replied indignantly, "A slug indeed! You better be careful how you treat me! For your information I am a puppet!"

"A puppet?" replied the fisherman. "To be honest, I'm not familiar with the puppet-fish species – so much the better! I'll eat you with greater relish."

"Eat me? But can't you understand that I'm not a fish? Can't you hear that I speak and reason like you?"

"That's absolutely true," agreed the fisherman, "and since I can see that you are a fish who is lucky enough to be able to speak and reason like me, I will indeed treat you with due respect."

"Which means what?"

"As a sign of my friendship and extraordinary esteem, I'll allow you to choose how you would like to be cooked. Would you prefer to be fried in a skillet, or would you rather be stewed in a pot with a tomato sauce?"

"To be honest," replied Pinocchio, "if I had to choose, I'd prefer to be set free instead, so I could go back home."

"Surely you jest! Do you think I'd miss out on tasting such a rare fish? It isn't every day that you find a puppet-fish in these waters. Trust me: I'll fry you up in a skillet together with all the other fishes, and you'll end up liking it. It's always comforting to be fried in company."

After this speech, the unhappy Pinocchio began to cry and scream and plead, and as he cried he said, "How much better it would have been if I had gone to school today! I listened to my schoolmates, and now I'm paying for it! Boo-hoo-hoo!"

And since he was wriggling like an eel and trying incredibly hard to slither out of the green fisherman's clutches, the fisherman took a nice length of reed, tied Pinocchio's hands and legs together like sausage ends, and threw him into the bucket with the others.

Then, taking out a battered wooden tray heaped with flour, he began flouring all those fish. And after he floured them, he threw them, one by one, into the sizzling skillet.

The first to dance in the boiling oil were the poor goatfish. The hake were next, then the sea bass, then the mullet, then the sole, then the anchovies, and then finally it was Pinocchio's turn. Seeing himself so close to death – and such a nasty death at that! – he began trembling so violently from fear that he had no voice or breath left for begging.

The poor boy begged with his eyes! But the green fisherman, not even noticing, rolled him five or six times in the flour, covering him so thoroughly from head to toe that he looked like a plaster puppet.

Then he took him by the head, and . . .

Chapter 29

Just as the fisherman was on the verge of tossing Pinocchio into the skillet, a large dog entered the cave, lured there by the pungent, appetizing aroma of frying fish.

"Get out!" shouted the fisherman menacingly, still holding the flour-covered puppet in his hand. But the poor dog was as hungry as four dogs, and his whimpering and tail-wagging seemed to say, "Give me a bite of fried fish and I'll leave you in peace."

"I said get out!" repeated the fisherman, and he pulled back his foot to give the dog a kick.

But this was a dog who, when he was truly hungry, did not take kindly to being trifled with, and he started growling at the fisherman and showing his terrible fangs.

At that moment a little voice called out faintly in the cave, "Save me, Wingfoot! If you don't save me, I'm going to fry!"

The dog recognized Pinocchio's voice at once, and to his great astonishment he realized that it was coming from that flour-coated bundle the fisherman held in his hand.

What could he do? He lunged mightily into the air, seized the flour-covered puppet in his mouth, and ran out of the cave holding it gently between his teeth – quick as a wink he was gone!

The fisherman, infuriated to see a fish that he would have happily eaten snatched from his hand, started to chase the dog. But after taking a few steps, he burst into a fit of coughing and had to turn back.

Meanwhile, having found once more the path that led to the village, Wingfoot stopped and set Pinocchio gently on the ground.

"I can't thank you enough!" said the puppet.

"No need to," replied the dog. "You saved me, and one good turn deserves another. After all, we must help one another in this world."

"But how on earth did you end up in that cave?"

"I was still lying on the beach, more dead than alive, when the aroma of frying fish wafted in on the wind. That aroma whetted my appetite, and I tracked it down. If I had arrived a minute later—"

"Don't even say it!" yelled Pinocchio, still trembling with fear. "Don't even say it! If you arrived a minute later then I'd be good and fried by now, eaten and digested – eek! I shudder at the thought!"

Wingfoot, laughing, held out his right paw to the puppet, who shook it long and hard as a sign of their close friendship. And then they went their separate ways.

The dog took the road back to the village. Pinocchio, on his own again, approached a nearby hut where a little old man in the doorway was sunning himself, and asked, "Tell me, kind sir, do you know anything about a poor boy named Eugenio who was wounded in the head?"

"The boy was brought by some fishermen to this hut, but now—"

"Now he's dead!" interjected Pinocchio, with great sorrow.

"No, now he's alive. He's already gone home."

"Really and truly?" shouted the puppet, jumping for joy. "So the wound wasn't serious?"

"Well, it could have been awfully serious, even fatal," replied the little old man, "because someone flung a big hardbound book at his head."

"And who flung it?"

"One of his schoolmates – a certain Pinocchio."

"And who is this Pinocchio?" the puppet asked, playing dumb.

"Folks say he's a good-for-nothing boy, a vagabond, a real hothead."

"Slander! It's all slander!"

"Are you acquainted with this Pinocchio?"

"I've seen him!" replied the puppet.

"And what's your estimation of him?" asked the little old man.

"To me, he seems like a fine upstanding lad – really likes to study, does as he's told, loves his daddy and his family . . ."

As the puppet was telling all these lies with a straight face, he touched his nose and realized that it had grown more than a handbreadth in length. Suddenly afraid, he began to shout, "Pay no attention, kind sir, to all the good things I've been saying about him. Because I know Pinocchio perfectly well and I too can assure you that he really is a lazy good-for-nothing boy who doesn't do as he's told and runs around with his schoolmates like a scamp!"

As soon as he said these words, his nose shortened back to its natural length, just as it was before.

"And why are you all white like that?"

"I can explain: I accidentally rubbed up against a wall that had just been whitewashed," replied the puppet, ashamed to admit he had been floured like a fish in preparation for frying in a skillet.

"And what have you done with your jacket, your shorts, your cap?"

"I ran into some thieves and they stripped me. Say, kind sir, you don't by any chance have any scraps of clothing you could give me, so that I could return home?"

"My boy, as far as clothes go, I've got nothing but a little sack I keep my lupini beans in. If you want it, take it – it's right over there."

Pinocchio didn't need to be told twice: he quickly took the lupini sack, which was empty, and after using some scissors to cut a small hole in the bottom and two on the sides, he put it on like a shirt. And dressed in this light fashion, he headed back to the village.

But on the way he felt ill at ease – so ill at ease, in fact, that he took one step backwards for every two steps forwards. And all the while he was talking to himself: "How can I ever show my face to the good Fairy? What will she say when she sees me? Will she forgive me this second escapade? I bet she won't forgive me! Oh, she certainly won't forgive me! And it serves me right! Because I'm a rascal, always making promises to change my ways and never keeping them!"

He arrived in the village after dark. And because the weather was bad – the rain was coming down in buckets – he went straight to the Fairy's house and resolved to knock on the door and ask to be let in.

But once he got there his courage deserted him, and instead of knocking he ran about twenty paces away. Then he approached the door a second time, but did nothing. He approached a third time: still he did nothing. The fourth time he took the knocker in his hand, trembling, and tapped softly.

He waited and waited and finally, after half an hour, a top-floor window opened (the house was four storeys high), and out leaned a large Snail with a glowing lantern on her head, and she said, "Who's there at this hour?"

"Is the Fairy home?" the puppet asked.

"The Fairy is sleeping and doesn't wish to be disturbed. But who's there?"

"It's me!"

"Me who?"

"Pinocchio."

"Pinocchio who?"

"The puppet, the one who lives with the Fairy."

"Oh, I see," said the Snail. "Wait right there – I'll come straight down to let you in."

"Please hurry, for heaven's sake – I'm dying of cold."

"My boy, I am a snail, and snails never hurry."

Meanwhile an hour passed, then two, but the door did not open. And so Pinocchio, trembling from being cold, afraid, and wet as a drowned rat, gathered his courage and knocked once more, and louder this time.

After the second knock, a window opened on the third floor, and the same Snail leaned out.

"Oh, pretty little Snail," shouted Pinocchio from the street, "I've been waiting for two hours! And two hours, on such an awful night, feel longer than two years. For heaven's sake, please hurry."

"My boy," that creature replied, calmly and coolly, "my boy, I am a snail, and snails never hurry."

And the window closed again.

Soon the bells chimed midnight. Then one o'clock. And then two. But the door remained shut. Losing his patience, Pinocchio grabbed the door knocker angrily, intending to bang it hard enough to shake the whole building. But the door knocker, which had been made of iron, suddenly turned into a live eel, which slithered out of his hands and disappeared into the torrent of water that was coursing down the street.

"So that's how it is!" shouted Pinocchio, blinded now by rage. "The knocker may have disappeared, but I can knock just fine with my feet."

And stepping back a little, he let fly with a tremendous kick. The blow was so hard, in fact, that his foot sank halfway into the wood, and when he tried to pull it back out, he couldn't budge it: his foot was stuck in that door like a hammered nail.

Imagine poor Pinocchio! He had to spend the rest of the night with one foot on the ground and the other up in the air.

In the morning, near dawn, the door finally opened. That good creature the Snail had taken only nine hours to descend from the fourth floor to the front door. It must be said that she had worked up a sweat.

"What's that foot of yours doing stuck in the door?" she asked the puppet with a laugh.

"It was an accident. Oh, pretty little Snail, could you help release me from this torture?"

"My boy, this calls for a carpenter, and I've never been much of a carpenter."

"Please beg the Fairy on my behalf!"

"The Fairy is sleeping and doesn't wish to be disturbed."

"But what am I supposed to do, nailed to this door all day?"

"Amuse yourself by counting the ants that pass by on the street."

"At least please bring me something to eat – I'm wasting away."

"At once!" said the Snail.

And indeed, three and a half hours later, she returned with a silver tray on her head. On the tray was bread, a roast chicken, and four ripe apricots.

"Here is the breakfast the Fairy sends you," said the Snail.

The puppet rejoiced at the sight of that heavenly gift. But when he took a bite, his spirits plummeted, for the bread was plaster, the chicken cardboard, and the four apricots alabaster – all painted to look real.

He wanted to weep, wanted to give himself up to despair, wanted to throw that tray and everything on it away. But what he did instead, either from his great sorrow or his great hunger, was to faint.

When he came to, he found himself stretched out on a sofa, the Fairy sitting next to him.

"I forgive you this time, too," the Fairy said. "But watch out: if you do this sort of thing to me again . . . !"

Pinocchio promised up and down that he would study and would behave himself from then on. And he kept his word for the whole rest of the school year. Indeed, when end-of-the-year exams came, he got the highest marks of anyone in the school. And his behaviour, in general, was judged so praiseworthy and satisfactory that the Fairy, delighted, told him, "Tomorrow your wish shall be granted at last!"

"What wish?"

"Tomorrow you'll stop being a puppet and become a proper boy."

No one who wasn't there to see Pinocchio's joy at this long-awaited news can quite imagine it. All his friends and schoolmates were to be invited to the Fairy's house the next morning for a grand breakfast, to help celebrate the great occasion, and the Fairy had prepared two hundred cups of coffee-and-milk, and four hundred rolls, buttered inside and out. The next day promised to be a beautiful and joyous one. *But* . . .

Alas, in the lives of puppets, there is always some *but* that spoils everything.

Chapter 30

Naturally, Pinocchio immediately asked the Fairy's permission to go around town to make the invitations. And the Fairy said, "Go ahead and invite your friends to tomorrow's breakfast, but remember to come home before dark. OK?"

"I promise to be back in an hour or so," replied the puppet.

"Careful, Pinocchio! Children are quick to make promises, but they're often slow to keep them."

"But I'm not like other children: when I say something, I stick to it."

"We'll see. If you don't, so much the worse for you."

"What do you mean?"

"I mean that children who ignore the advice of those who know best always get themselves into some kind of trouble."

"As I know from experience!" said Pinocchio. "But I'll never be guilty of such folly again!"

"We'll see if you're right."

With that, the puppet said goodbye to the good Fairy, who was a sort of mother to him, and sang and danced his way out of the house.

In little more than an hour, all his friends had been invited. Some accepted quickly and eagerly; others played hard to get at first, but when they heard that the rolls for dunking in the coffee-and-milk would be buttered even on the outside, they all ended up saying, "We're coming, too, as a favour to you."

Now you need to know that, among Pinocchio's schoolmates, his dearest, closest friend was a boy whose name was Romeo, but everyone called him by his nickname, Lampwick, on account of his skinny, lanky build – as skinny as a fresh wick in a night lamp.

Lampwick was the laziest and naughtiest boy in the whole school, but Pinocchio loved him dearly. In fact he had gone straight to his house to look for him, to invite him to the breakfast, but he couldn't find him. He went back once more; Lampwick wasn't there. He went back a third time, but again no luck.

How could he track him down? He looked here, he looked there – then finally he saw him hiding under the porch of a farmer's house.

"What are you doing there?" Pinocchio asked as he approached.

"I'm waiting to leave."

"Where are you going?"

"Far, far, far away!"

"And here I've been to your house three times looking for you!"

"What do you want with me?"

"Don't you know about the big event? Don't you know about my good fortune?"

"What is it?"

"Tomorrow I'll stop being a puppet and become a boy, like you, like all the others."

"I hope it makes you happy."

"Tomorrow, then, I'll expect you for breakfast at my house."

"But what if I told you I was leaving tonight?"

"At what time?"

"Soon."

"And where are you going?"

"I'm going to live in a land – in the most beautiful land on earth. A real paradise!"

"And what's it called?"

"It's called Toyland. Why don't you come too?"

"Me? No way!"

"Big mistake, Pinocchio! Believe me, if you don't come, you'll regret it. Where will you find a place that's better for us kids? There are no schools, no teachers and no books there. In that blessed land, no one ever studies. There isn't any school on Thursdays, and every week is made up of six Thursdays and one Sunday. Just think: the winter holidays start on the first day of January and they end on the last day of December. Now that's my kind of place! That's how it should be in every civilized country!"

"But how do people spend their days in Toyland?"

"They spend them playing and having fun from morning to night. Then at night they go to bed, and the next morning they start all over. What do you think?"

"Hmm!" said Pinocchio, nodding his head, as if to say: "That's a life I too could enjoy!"

"So, do you want to leave with me? Yes or no? Make up your mind."

"No, no, no, and again no. I've promised my good Fairy to become a proper boy, and I want to keep my word. In fact, since I see that the sun's going down, I must leave you at once and run off. Goodbye, then, and happy travels."

"Where are you running in such a hurry?"

"Home. My good Fairy wants me to be back before dark."

"Wait another two minutes."

"I'm already running late."

"Just two minutes."

"And what if the Fairy yells at me?"

"Let her yell. After she's had a good yell, she'll calm down," said that rascal Lampwick.

"And how are you getting there? Are you leaving alone, or with others?"

"Alone? There'll be more than a hundred of us kids."

"And you're travelling on foot?"

"A coach will come to pick me up and take me across the border into that happy country."

"Oh, I wish I could see that coach pass by now!"

"Why?"

"To see all of you leave together."

"Wait around a bit longer and you'll see it."

"No, no – I want to go home."

"Wait two more minutes."

"I've already lingered too long. The Fairy will be worried about me."

"Poor Fairy! I guess maybe she's scared you'll get eaten by bats?"

"But tell me," Pinocchio said, "are you really sure that in that country there are no schools at all?"

"Not even the shadow of a school."

"And no teachers, either?"

"Not a single one."

"And you never have to study?"

"Never, never, never!"

"Oh, what a splendid country!" said Pinocchio, feeling his mouth begin to water. "What a splendid country! I haven't ever been there, but I can picture it!"

"Why don't you come, too?"

"It's pointless for you to tempt me! I've already promised my good Fairy that I'd become a sensible boy, and I don't want to break my promise."

"Farewell then, and give my best regards to the primary schools – and the secondary schools, too, if you pass them on the street!"

"Farewell, Lampwick. Have a good trip, enjoy yourself, and think of your friends from time to time."

Having said that, the puppet took two steps towards home. But then, stopping and turning back towards his friend, he asked, "But are you really positive that every week is made up of six Thursdays and one Sunday?"

"Absolutely positive."

"And you're certain that vacations start on the first day of January and end on the last day of December?"

"Absolutely certain."

"What a splendid country!" repeated Pinocchio, so overwhelmed by delight that he spat. Then he made up his mind and quickly added: "Well, it really is goodbye: happy travels."

"Farewell."

"When will you be leaving?"

"Soon!"

"I'm very nearly tempted to wait."

"But what about the Fairy?"

"At this point, I'm already running late! One hour more or less won't make any difference."

"Poor Pinocchio! What if the Fairy yells at you?"

"Never mind! I'll let her yell. After she's had a good yell, she'll calm down."

It was already dark, pitch-dark, by the time they saw a small light moving in the distance and heard the sound of harness bells and the blare of a toy trumpet, so faint and muffled that it sounded like the whine of a mosquito!

"It's here!" shouted Lampwick, getting to his feet.

"What is?" asked Pinocchio in a soft voice.

"The coach that's coming to pick me up. So, do you want to come: yes or no?"

"But is it really true," asked the puppet, "that children in that country are never required to study?"

"Never, never, never!"

"What a splendid country! What a splendid country! What a splendid country!"

Chapter 31

At last the coach arrived. And it arrived without making the slightest noise because its wheels were wrapped with tow and rags.

The coach was drawn by twelve pairs of donkeys, uniformly small in size but various in colour.

Some had brown fur, some had white fur, some had salt-and-pepper speckling, and some had large yellow-and-blue stripes.

But the strangest thing was this: that those twelve pairs of donkeys – those twenty-four donkeys – instead of wearing horseshoes like all other beasts of burden, were wearing boots of white leather.

And the coachman?

Picture a miniature man wider than he was tall, as soft and oily as a pat of butter, with a face like a little rose apple, a little mouth that was always laughing, and a thin, unctuous voice, like a wheedling cat appealing to its kind mistress.

All the children adored him as soon as they saw him, and they raced to climb into his coach, to be taken to that paradise on earth that goes by the name of Toyland on the maps.

Indeed the coach was already chock full of kids between the ages of eight and twelve, packed one on top of the other like pickled sardines. They were uncomfortable, they were squished, they could scarcely breathe – but not a single one said *ouch!* or complained at all. The comfort of knowing that in a few hours they would arrive in a country without books or school or teachers made them so happy and agreeable that they felt neither sore, nor strained, nor hungry, nor thirsty, nor sleepy.

As soon as the coach had stopped, Mini-Man turned to Lampwick, all smirks and courtesy, and asked with a smile, "Tell me, my fine boy, do you too wish to travel to that happy country?"

"I certainly do."

"Well, I must warn you, my dear, there's no more room in the coach. As you can see, it's all full!"

"No problem," replied Lampwick. "If there's no room inside, I'll make do by riding on the harness shafts."

And with a leap, he climbed up onto the shafts.

"And you, my sweet," said Mini-Man, turning ceremoniously to Pinocchio. "What do you intend to do? Are you coming with us, or staying here?"

"I'm staying," replied Pinocchio. "I want to go back home. I want to study and I want to do well in school, as all proper boys do."

"I hope it makes you happy!"

Then Lampwick said, "Pinocchio, listen to me: come with us, and we'll have fun."

"No, no, no!"

"Come with us and we'll have fun!" shouted several other voices from inside the coach.

"Come with us and we'll have fun!" screamed all the children in chorus – it seemed like a hundred voices.

"And if I come with you, what will I tell my good Fairy?" said the puppet, who was beginning to weaken and waver.

"Don't worry your head with such gloomy stuff. Just think, we're going to a land where we'll be free to raise a ruckus from morning to night!"

Pinocchio didn't reply, but he sighed. Then he sighed again. Then a third time. Finally he said, "Make a little room – I'm coming too!"

"The seats are all taken," replied Mini-Man,"but to show you how welcome you are, I'll let you take my driver's seat."

"What about you?"

"I'll go on foot."

"No, I couldn't allow that. I'd rather ride on the back of one of these little donkeys!"

And just like that he approached the front pair of donkeys and tried to mount the one on the right. But the creature, turning abruptly, rammed him hard in the stomach and knocked him head over heels.

Imagine the mischievous, boisterous laughter of all those kids who were watching.

But Mini-Man didn't laugh. Full of tenderness, he approached the little rebellious donkey and, pretending to give it a kiss, bit off half of its right ear.

Meanwhile Pinocchio, having angrily picked himself up off the ground, leapt high in the air and onto that poor creature's back. It was such a splendid leap that the children stopped laughing at him and began shouting *Hurray for Pinocchio!* and applauding so

wildly it seemed they might never stop.

But suddenly the little donkey raised both its back legs off the ground and bucked violently, flinging the poor puppet into the middle of the road, onto a pile of gravel.

More rowdy laughter. But Mini-Man, instead of laughing, was overcome by such affection for that restless little donkey that, with a kiss, he bit half of its other ear cleanly off. Then he told the puppet, "Go ahead and get back on – nothing to fear. That little donkey had a bee in his bonnet, but I whispered a word or two in his ears, and now I expect he'll be tame and reasonable."

Pinocchio mounted. And the coach began to move. But as the donkeys galloped and the coach sped over the cobblestones of the main road, the puppet thought he heard a soft, barely audible voice that said, "Poor sap! You wanted to do as you pleased, but you'll regret it!"

Pinocchio, a little spooked, looked here and there, trying to figure out where those words were coming from. But he couldn't see anyone. The donkeys were galloping, the coach was racing along, the children inside the coach were sleeping, Lampwick was snoring like a saw, and Mini-Man, sitting in his driver's seat, was singing under his breath:

"Everybody sleeps at night
But I don't sleep at all . . ."

After another half a kilometre, Pinocchio heard the same faint little voice telling him, "Keep in mind, you simpleton, that kids who stop studying and turn their backs on books and schools and teachers to devote themselves to toys and fun, they always come to grief! Take it from me; I know from experience! The day will come when you'll regret it, too, as I regret it now – but then it will be too late!"

At these softly whispered words, the puppet, more scared than ever, jumped down off the back of his donkey and seized it by the muzzle.

Imagine how he felt when he saw that his little donkey was crying – and crying just like a child!

"Hey, Mr Mini-Man," shouted Pinocchio to the coachman, "do you know what's going on here? This little donkey is crying."

"Let him cry – on his wedding day he'll laugh."

"Was it you by chance who taught him to talk?"

"No, he learned to stammer a few words on his own, from spending three years in the company of trained dogs."

"Poor beast!"

"Come, now," said Mini-Man, "let's not waste our time crying for a donkey. Mount him again and let's go – the night is cool and the road is long."

Pinocchio obeyed without another word. The coach resumed its course, and in the morning, near dawn, they happily reached Toyland.

This country resembled no other country in the world. Its population was composed entirely of children. The oldest were fourteen years of age; the youngest were barely eight. In the streets, such joy, such racket, such screeching as might take the top of your head off! Hordes of rascals everywhere. Some were playing ball, some marbles, some bowls; some were riding bicycles, others wooden horses; some were playing blindman's buff, some tag; some, dressed as clowns, were eating fire; some were acting, some singing, some doing flips; some amused themselves by walking with their hands on the ground and their feet in the air; some rolled hoops; some strolled about dressed as generals, with newspaper helmets and papier-mâché swords; some laughed, some yelled, some called to friends; some clapped and some whistled and some clucked like hens that had just laid eggs – such a pandemonium, in other words, such a din, such an infernal hullabaloo, that you'd have to stuff your ears with cotton to keep from going deaf. Every square hosted little canvas theatres that were packed with kids from dawn till dusk, and the walls of every house bore phrases scrawled in charcoal that said splendid things like: *Toys are grate!* (instead of great), *No more skools!* (instead of schools), *Down with Ritt Matick!* (instead of arithmetic), and other such gems.

As for Pinocchio and Lampwick and all the other children who had made the journey with Mini-Man, as soon as they set foot in town they plunged right into the heart of that great hubbub, and in a matter of minutes, as you might well guess, they had made friends with everyone. Who could have been happier, who more contented, than they? Amid that continuous fun and those various amusements, the hours and days and weeks passed like so many flashes of lightning.

"Oh, what a beautiful life!" said Pinocchio every time he happened to run into Lampwick.

"You see, was I right or what?" Lampwick always replied. "And to think you didn't want to come! To think that you had gotten it into your head to go back home to your Fairy, to waste your time studying! If you're now free from the boredom of books and school, you owe it to me, to my advice, to my kindness – don't you think? Only our truest friends can do us such great favours."

"It's true, Lampwick! If I'm a truly happy boy today, it's all thanks to you. Our teacher, though – you know what he used to say about you? He always said, 'Don't spend time with that scamp Lampwick, because he's a bad influence and will only lead you astray!'"

"Poor teacher!" replied Lampwick, shaking his head. "I know all too well that he didn't care for me, and that he always liked to slander me. But I'm generous and I forgive him!"

"Noble soul!" said Pinocchio, warmly embracing his friend and giving him a kiss on the forehead.

This fine paradise of nothing but fun and games all the livelong day, with no books or schools in sight, went on for five months, until one morning Pinocchio woke to discover, as the saying goes, a rather nasty surprise, which left him in a bad mood indeed.

Chapter 32

And what might this surprise be?

I'll tell you, my dear little readers: the surprise was that Pinocchio, when he woke up, naturally gave his head a scratch, and as he was scratching, he noticed—

Well, can you guess what he noticed?

He noticed, to his great shock, that his ears were now bigger than his hands.

All his life, you see, the puppet had had tiny little ears – so tiny they couldn't be seen with the naked eye! So imagine his reaction when he touched his ears and found that, during the night, they had grown so long they looked like two leaves on a corn stalk.

He immediately went to find a mirror, so he could look at himself. Failing to find one, he filled the washbasin with water, and looking down at his reflection he saw something he would rather never have seen: his own image adorned with a magnificent pair of donkey ears.

I'll leave it to you to imagine poor Pinocchio's sorrow, shame, and despair!

He began to cry, to shriek, to bang his head against the wall. But the more he despaired, the more the ears grew and grew and grew, and they were becoming furry at their tips.

At the sound of those piercing cries, his door opened and in came a pretty little Marmot, who lived upstairs from him, and who, seeing the puppet in such a frenzy, asked him gently, "What's wrong, my dear housemate?"

"I'm sick, my dear Marmot, very sick – and sick with a sickness that scares me! Do you know anything about pulses?"

"A little."

"Then check mine, to see if by chance I have a fever."

The Marmot raised her right forepaw, and after taking Pinocchio's pulse, she said to him with a sigh, "My friend, I'm afraid I have some bad news!"

"What is it?"

"You have a terrible fever!"

"What kind of fever?"

"Jackass fever."

"I don't understand what jackass fever is!" said the puppet, though alas he did understand.

"I'll explain it, then," said the Marmot. "You should know that within two or three hours you'll no longer be a puppet, or even a little boy."

"Then what will I be?"

"Within two or three hours, you'll become a real live donkey, like the ones who pull the coaches and carry heads of cabbage and lettuce to market."

"Oh, poor me! Poor me!" cried Pinocchio, seizing both ears in his hands and tugging them and yanking them furiously, as if they were someone else's ears.

"My dear," replied the Marmot, trying to comfort him, "what can you do about it now? It's your destiny. It's written among the decrees of wisdom that all those lazy children who, bored with books and school and teachers, spend their days playing games and having fun will sooner or later end up turning into little jackasses."

"Is that really true?" asked the puppet, sobbing.

"Unfortunately it is! So there's no use crying now. You should have thought of that sooner!"

"But it's not my fault, believe me: it's all Lampwick's fault!"

"And who is this Lampwick?"

"A schoolmate of mine. I wanted to go home, I wanted to do as I was told, I wanted to keep studying and do well in school – but Lampwick said, 'Why bother studying? Why go to school? Come with me instead, to Toyland. There, we won't have to study any more. There, we'll have fun from dusk till dawn and we'll always be happy.'"

"And why did you listen to the advice of that false friend, that bad influence?"

"Why? Because, my dear Marmot, I'm a foolish and heartless puppet. Oh! If I had any heart at all, I never would have abandoned that good Fairy, who loved me like a mother and who did so much for me! And then, instead of a puppet, I'd now be a respectable boy, like so many others! Oh, if I run into that Lampwick, he better be careful – I'm going to give him an earful!"

He turned to go. But on reaching the door he remembered he had donkey ears. Since he was ashamed to show them in public, do you know what he did? He put on a big nightcap and pulled it so far down on his head that it nearly touched his nose.

He then went out and started looking all over for Lampwick. He looked in the streets, in the squares, in the theatres – everywhere. But he couldn't find him. He asked everyone he saw, but no one had seen him.

He decided to try Lampwick's house. Once at the door, he knocked.

"Who is it?" asked Lampwick from within.

"It's me!" replied the puppet.

"Just a minute, I'll open the door."

Half an hour later, the door opened. Imagine Pinocchio's reaction when, entering the room, he saw his friend Lampwick wearing a big nightcap pulled down to his nose.

The sight of that nightcap almost made Pinocchio feel better, and he immediately wondered: "Might my friend have the same sickness I do? Might he, too, be suffering from donkey fever?"

Smiling and pretending not to notice anything, he asked, "How are you, my dear Lampwick?"

"I feel great, like a mouse in a wheel of parmesan cheese."

"Do you really mean it?"

"Why would I lie to you?"

"Excuse me, my friend – but why then are you wearing that nightcap, which covers both your ears?"

"Doctor's orders – I injured my knee. And you, dear Pinocchio, why are you wearing that nightcap, which has been tugged down to your nose?"

"Doctor's orders – I scraped my foot."

"Oh, poor Pinocchio!"

"Oh, poor Lampwick!"

A long silence followed these words, during which the two friends did nothing but look mockingly at each other.

At last the puppet, in a soft, sweet voice, said to his friend, "I'm curious, my dear Lampwick: have you ever had any problems with your ears?"

"Never! And you?"

"Never! Ever since this morning, though, one of my ears has been aching."

"I've got the same pain myself."

"You, too? And which ear is the one that hurts?"

"Both of them. And you?"

144

"Both of them. Could it be the same sickness?"

"I'm afraid it might be."

"Would you do me a favour, Lampwick?"

"Gladly! With all my heart."

"Show me your ears?"

"Why not? But first I want to see yours, my dear Pinocchio."

"No, you have to go first."

"No, dear: you first, then me!"

"Well then," said the puppet, "let's make a deal, like good friends."

"Let's hear the deal."

"We'll both take off our hats at the same time – agreed?"

"Agreed."

"OK, get ready!"

And Pinocchio began to count out loud: "One! Two! Three!"

At the word *three!* the two boys grabbed their hats and threw them into the air.

The scene that followed might seem unbelievable were it not true. Pinocchio and Lampwick, when each saw that the other was stricken with the same misfortune, instead of being mortified and sorrowful, began poking fun at each other's outsized ears until, after a thousand incivilities, they wound up bursting into hearty laughter.

And they laughed and they laughed until they were doubled over with laughter. But suddenly, at the height of their hilarity, Lampwick stopped laughing and began to stagger and to change colour, and he said to his friend, "Help, Pinocchio, help!"

"What's wrong?"

"Oh no! I can no longer stand up straight."

"Neither can I," shouted Pinocchio, crying and tottering.

And as they spoke, they both fell forwards onto all fours and began to trot and run around the room on their hands and feet. And as they ran, their hands became hoofs, their faces lengthened into muzzles, and their backs grew a coat of light brown fur speckled with black.

But do you know what the worst moment was for those two wretches? The worst, most humiliating moment was when they felt their tails sprouting behind them. Overcome then by shame and by pain, they tried to weep and to lament their fate.

If only they had never tried that! Because instead of moans and laments, out came the braying of jackasses. And they brayed resoundingly, in chorus: *hee-haw, hee-haw, hee-haw.*

Just then there was a knock at the door, and they heard a voice outside say, "Open up! Mini-Man here, the coachman who brought you to this country. Open up at once, or else!"

Chapter 33

When no one opened the door, Mini-Man opened it wide with a violent kick. Entering the room, he addressed Pinocchio and Lampwick with his usual giggle, saying, "Well done, boys! You brayed nicely, and I recognized your voices right away. And so here I am."

At these words, the hearts of those two little donkeys sank, their heads bowed, their ears drooped, and their tails slid between their legs.

First Mini-Man rubbed them, stroked them, patted them. Then he took out his currycomb and began thoroughly grooming them. After combing them until they gleamed like two mirrors, he put halters on them and led them to the market square, in hopes of selling them and pocketing a tidy sum.

And indeed he did not have to wait for buyers.

A farmer whose jackass had died the day before bought Lampwick, and Pinocchio was sold to the Ringmaster of a troupe of clowns and acrobats, who planned to train him to jump and dance with the other beasts in his troupe.

And now do you understand, my little readers, what a fine line of work Mini-Man was in? This nasty little monstrosity, who looked all milk and honey, went about the world from time to time in his coach, using promises and sweet talk to gather up all the lazy children who were bored with books and school. And after loading them into his coach, he drove them to Toyland and let them spend all their time playing, raising a ruckus, and having fun.

And when those poor deluded children, as a consequence of always playing and never studying, turned into so many donkeys, well then Mini-Man, pleased as punch, would seize them and take them off to fairs and markets to be sold. And so, in just a few years, he had made scads of money and become a millionaire.

What became of Lampwick I can't say. I do know, however, that Pinocchio's new life was, from the very beginning, gruelling and harsh.

When he was led to his stall, his new master filled the manger with chopped straw. But Pinocchio, after tasting a mouthful, spat it back out.

So his master, grumbling, filled the manger with hay — but Pinocchio didn't like hay, either.

"Oh, so you don't like hay, either?" shouted his master angrily. "Don't worry, my pretty little donkey, if you've got some silly notions into your head, I'll be sure to get them out!" And to teach him a lesson, he smacked his whip across his legs.

The sharp pain caused Pinocchio to cry and bray, and braying he said, *"Hee-haw, hee-haw,* I can't digest straw!"

"So eat hay then!" replied his master, who understood asinine dialect quite well.

"Hee-haw, hee-haw, hay makes my tummy ache!"

"I suppose you expect me to feed a jackass like yourself on breast of chicken and galantine of capon?" replied his owner, becoming angrier and angrier and smacking him again with his whip.

After this second lashing, Pinocchio wisely held his tongue and said no more.

When the stable door was closed, Pinocchio was left alone. And since he hadn't eaten in many hours, he began to yawn from hunger. And when he yawned, his mouth opened as wide as an oven.

Finally, finding nothing else in the manger, he resigned himself to chewing a bit of hay. And after having chewed it really well, he closed his eyes and gulped it down.

"This hay isn't that bad," he thought to himself, "but how much better things would be if I had kept studying! Right now, instead of hay, I could be eating a hunk of fresh bread and a nice slice of salami! Oh well!"

When he woke the next morning, he immediately looked in the manger for more hay, but he found none, having eaten it all during the night.

So he then took a bite of the chopped straw, and as he stood there chewing it he had to admit that chopped straw tasted nothing like either Milanese rice or Neapolitan macaroni.

"Oh well!" he repeated, still chewing. "But I hope at least that my misfortune can be a lesson to all those disobedient kids who don't want to study. Oh well! Oh well!"

"Oh well, my foot!" yelled his master, entering the stable at that very moment. "Do you think, my pretty little donkey, that I bought you just to offer you food and drink? I bought you so you'll work and earn me a handsome profit. Come on, now, attaboy! Come with me to the circus and I'll teach you how to jump through hoops, how to smash cardboard barrels with your head, and how to dance the waltz and the polka up on your hind legs."

Whether he liked it or not, poor Pinocchio had to learn all these fine things. But it took three months of lessons to learn them, and nearly enough whippings to take his hide off.

At last the day came when his master could announce a truly extraordinary event. Notices of various colours, posted on street corners, said this:

GRAND GALA SHOW

~

This evening
WITNESS THE TROUPE'S USUAL
AMAZING LEAPS & FEATS
PERFORMED BY ALL ITS ARTISTS
& all its horses, mares and stallions alike,

plus

appearing for the first time
the famous
DONKEY PINOCCHIO
also known as
THE STAR OF THE DANCE

~

The theatre will be as bright as day

That evening, as you might guess, the theatre was already jam-packed an hour before the show was to begin.

Not a single seat was left, not in the orchestra, not in the boxes, not even if you could afford to pay its weight in gold.

Around the circus, the tiers of seats were teeming with children, children of all ages, who were in a frenzy of excitement to see the famous Donkey Pinocchio dance.

When the first portion of the show came to an end, the Ringmaster, dressed in a black tailcoat, tight white trousers, and knee-high leather boots, introduced himself to the packed audience, and after a sweeping bow he solemnly intoned the following preposterous speech: "Esteemed public, lords and ladies! Yours truly, whilst traversing through your illustrious metropolitan, wished to procreate for myself the honour, not to make mention of the pleasure, of presenting to such a discerning and distinct audience this famous donkey, who has heretofore enjoyed the honour of dancing in the presence of His Majesty the Emperor of all the major Courts of Europe. And albeit full of gratitude, please assist us with your arousing presence and indulge us!"

This speech was received with much laughter and much applause. But the applause redoubled and became a sort of hurricane as Donkey Pinocchio approached the centre of the ring. He was all decked out for the occasion: a new bridle of patent leather with brass buckles and studs, a white camellia blossom behind each ear, his mane divided up into lots of locks tied with charming white silk bows, and ribbons of green-and-red velvet braided into his tail. In short, he was an utterly adorable little donkey!

The Ringmaster continued his introduction of Pinocchio with these remarks: "Honourable auditors! I shall not stand here deceiving you with regard to the great difficulties surmounted by myself in captivating and subjugating the aforementioned mammal, whilst he grazed freely from mountaintop to mountaintop in the torrid zone. Observe, if you please, the wildness oozing forth from his eyes, notwithstanding our futile attempts to tame him to the life of a civilized quadruped, which oftentimes forced myself to resort to the genial parlance of the whip. But each kindness of mine, instead of endearing myself to him, made him even furthermore ill-disposed towards myself. Howsoever, following the Gallic system, I located within his cranium a small bony part, which that famous medicinal school in Paree has recognized as the bulb that regenerates hair and the Pyrrhic dance. And I absolved thenceforth to train him to dance, not to mention jump through hoops and paper-lined barrels. Marvel at him! And then judge him! But before I bid you much ado, allow me, ladies and gentlemen, to invite you back to the matinee show tomorrow evening. In the event that rainy weather threatens precipitation, the show will be postponed from tomorrow evening to eleven a.m. tomorrow afternoon."

And here the Ringmaster made another very deep bow. Then, turning to Pinocchio, he said, "Attaboy, Pinocchio! Before commencing your exploits, please greet our distinguished audience, lords, ladies, and children!"

Pinocchio obeyed at once, kneeling down on his two front knees and waiting until the Ringmaster, cracking his whip, shouted, "Walk!"

At that, the little donkey rose up on four legs and began to circle the ring, at a walking pace.

After a little while the Ringmaster said, "Trot!"

And Pinocchio, as instructed, quickened his pace into a trot.

"Canter!"

And Pinocchio began running.

"Gallop!"

And Pinocchio began racing as fast as he could. As he sped along like a Barbary steed, the Ringmaster raised his arm into the air and fired his pistol.

At the shot, the donkey, pretending to be hit, collapsed onto the ground and acted as if he were truly dying.

He got back to his feet amid an explosion of applause and cheers that seemed to him to rise up to the sky, and so, naturally, he lifted his head to look up. And looking up, he saw in one of the boxes a beautiful lady with a thick gold chain around her neck, from which hung a medallion. On the medallion was painted the portrait of a puppet.

"That's a portrait of me! That lady is the Fairy!" Pinocchio said to himself, for he recognized her at once. Overcome by happiness, he began to shout, "Oh, dear Fairy! Oh, dear Fairy!"

But instead of words, there emerged from his throat a bray so sonorous and sustained that it made every spectator in the theatre laugh, especially the children.

But the Ringmaster, to teach him the lesson that it wasn't good behaviour to start braying at the audience, gave him a whack on the nose with the handle of his whip.

Sticking his tongue way out, the poor donkey licked his nose for a good five minutes, thinking that perhaps that would ease the pain.

But imagine his despair when, turning back towards the audience, he saw that the Fairy's box was empty – she was gone!

He felt like dying; his eyes filled with tears and he began to sob. Nobody noticed, however, least of all the Ringmaster, who in fact cracked his whip and shouted, "Attaboy, Pinocchio! Now show these ladies and gentlemen how gracefully you can jump through hoops."

Pinocchio tried two or three times, but each time he approached the hoop, instead of jumping through it, he found it easier to go under it.

Finally he leapt into the air and through. Unfortunately, however, his back legs got caught on the hoop, causing him to crash to the ground in a heap on the other side.

When he got to his feet, he was limping, and he could barely walk back to the stable.

"Bring out Pinocchio! We want the Donkey! Bring out the Donkey!" shouted all the children from the orchestra seats, moved to pity by the wretched turn of events.

But the Donkey was not to be seen again that evening.

The next morning, after examining him, the veterinarian (that's a fancy word for animal doctor) declared that Pinocchio would be lame for the rest of his life.

At that the Ringmaster said to his stableboy, "What am I supposed to do with a lame donkey? He'd be nothing but a troublesome freeloader. Take him to the market and sell him."

Once they reached the market square, they quickly found a buyer, who asked the stableboy, "How much do you want for that lame donkey?"

"Twenty pounds."

"I'll give you twenty pennies. Don't pretend I'm buying him to work for me – I'm just buying him for his hide. I see that he's got really tough skin, and I want to make a drum out of it for my town's band."

I'll leave it to you, children, to guess how good Pinocchio felt when he heard he was destined to become a drum!

And indeed the buyer, as soon as he had paid his twenty pennies, led the donkey to the seashore. Then, after hanging a large stone around his neck and tying a rope to one of his feet, he gave him a quick shove, knocking him into the water.

With that stone around his neck, Pinocchio sank right to the bottom. And the buyer, holding the other end of the rope, sat down on a rock to wait until the donkey had had plenty of time to drown. Then he would skin him and go home with his hide.

Chapter 34

After the donkey had been under water for almost an hour, the buyer said, to nobody but himself, "By now my poor lame donkey must be good and drowned. Let's pull him back up so we can make a nice drum from his hide."

So he began to pull on the rope that he had tied to the donkey's leg. He pulled and pulled and pulled, and finally, breaking the surface of the water, he saw – can you guess? He saw, instead of a dead donkey, a live puppet, squirming like an eel.

Seeing that wooden puppet, the poor man thought he must be dreaming and he stood there dumbfounded, his mouth hanging open and his eyes popping out.

When he had collected himself a little, he wept and stammered and said, "And the donkey I threw into the sea – what happened to him?"

"That donkey was me!" replied the puppet, laughing.

"You?"

"Me."

"Oh, you scamp! You think you can play tricks on me?"

"Play tricks? Not at all, dear master. I'm being serious."

"But how in the world can a donkey, after spending a little time in the water, turn into a wooden puppet?"

"The salt water must have done it. The sea plays funny tricks."

"Careful, puppet! Don't think you can amuse yourself at my expense! Careful I don't lose my temper!"

"Well, master, do you want to learn the true story? Untie my leg and I'll tell you."

Curious to know the true story, that poor fool of a buyer quickly untied the knot that held the puppet fast, and Pinocchio, finding himself free as a bird, began to tell his story.

"So you see, I used to be a wooden puppet, as I am today. And I was just about to become a real boy, like so many others in this world, but instead I ran away from home, because I wasn't crazy about studying and because I was listening to my ne'er-do-well friends. And then one fine day I woke up to find myself turned into a jackass, ears and all – right down to the tail! I was so ashamed! I wouldn't want blessed Saint Anthony to make anyone, even you, feel such shame! Then I was taken to the donkey market and sold to

the Ringmaster of a horse circus, who got the notion to turn me into a great dancer and hoop-jumper. But one evening, during the show, I had a bad fall in the ring and injured two of my legs. So the Ringmaster, not knowing what to do with a lame donkey, sent me back to market, and then you bought me!"

"Alas! And I paid twenty pennies! And now who's going to give me back my money?"

"And why did you buy me? You bought me to make a drum out of my hide! A drum!"

"Alas! And now where will I find another hide?"

"Don't despair, master. There's no shortage of donkeys in this world."

"Tell me, you cheeky rascal, does your story end here?"

"No," replied the puppet, "just a few more words and then it will be over. After buying me, you led me to this place to kill me, but then, giving in to a humane, merciful impulse, you decided instead to hang a stone around my neck and throw me to the bottom of the sea. That softhearted impulse is a great credit to you, and I'll always be grateful to you for it. But this time, dear master, you didn't count on the Fairy."

"What Fairy is this?"

"She's my mother, and she's like all those good mothers who dote on their children and always keep an eye on them and come to their aid in times of trouble, even when those children, thanks to carelessness or bad behaviour, deserve to be abandoned and left to fend for themselves. So, as I was saying, the good Fairy, when she saw me in danger of drowning, sent a school of fish my way, and the fish, believing I actually was a dead donkey, started eating me! And what bites they took! I never would have believed that fish were greedier than children! Some ate my ears, some ate my muzzle, some my neck and some my mane, some ate the skin off my legs, some ate the fur off my back – and one among them was even kind enough to eat my tail."

"From now on," said the horrified buyer, "I swear never to eat a bite of fish again. I couldn't bear cutting open a goatfish or some fried hake and finding a donkey tail inside!"

"I agree," replied the puppet, laughing. "Besides, you should know that when the fishes finished eating away all of the asinine flesh that was covering me from head to toe, they finally got down to the bone – or rather down to the wood, because, as you can see, I'm made of extremely hard wood. After a few nibbles of that, those greedy fishes soon figured out that wood was not their cup of tea, and nauseated by such indigestible fare they swam off, some this way and some that way, without so much as a thank you. And now

I've told you how it came to pass that you found a live puppet at the end of your rope, instead of a dead donkey."

"I couldn't care less about your story," shouted the enraged buyer. "All I know is I paid twenty pennies for you, and I want my money back. You know what I'll do? I'll take you straight back to the market and sell you, by weight, as seasoned wood, good for starting fires."

"Go ahead, sell me again, I don't mind," said Pinocchio.

But as he said that, he leapt high into the air and splashed into the water. Swimming cheerfully away from the beach, he shouted back to the poor buyer, "Goodbye, master. If you ever need a hide to make a drum, think of me."

He laughed and kept on swimming. A minute later, he turned again and shouted even louder, "Goodbye, master. If you ever need some seasoned wood to start a fire, think of me."

And so it was that, before long, he had swum so far out that he was scarcely visible from shore. Or rather, all that was visible was a little black dot on the surface of the sea, a dot that every now and then lifted its legs out of the water to jump up and do flips, like a dolphin in a frisky mood.

As he swam about aimlessly, Pinocchio saw in the midst of the sea a rock that looked like white marble, and on top of it a pretty little goat was bleating affectionately and beckoning him to come near.

But the strangest thing was this: the goat's fleece, instead of being white or black or splotched with more than one colour, like the fleece of other goats, was completely blue – indeed it was such a dazzling sky-blue that it reminded him strongly of the Beautiful Girl.

I'll let you guess whether or not Pinocchio's heart began to beat faster! With renewed strength and energy, he began swimming towards the white rock, and he was already halfway there when he saw, rising out of the water and coming towards him, the terrifying head of a sea monster, its mouth gaping like a huge cavern, and three rows of fangs that would have been scary even just in a picture.

And do you know who this sea monster was?

This sea monster was none other than the gigantic Shark who was mentioned several times earlier in this story and who, thanks to his butchery and his insatiable voracity,

was known as "the Attila of fish and fishermen".

Imagine poor Pinocchio's dread at the sight of this monster. He tried to dodge him, to change directions. He tried to escape. But that enormous gaping mouth kept coming at him, fast as an arrow.

"Hurry, Pinocchio, for goodness' sake!" bleated the beautiful goat.

And Pinocchio swam desperately, using his arms, his chest, his legs, and his feet.

"Quick, Pinocchio, the monster's getting closer!"

And Pinocchio, gathering all his strength, swam even harder.

"Careful, Pinocchio! The monster's catching up! It's right there, it's right there! Hurry up, for goodness' sake, or you'll be lost!"

And Pinocchio swam faster than he ever had, on and on and on, zooming like a bullet. He was already nearly in reach of the rock, and the goat was already leaning out over the sea, stretching her forelegs towards him to help him out of the water . . .

But!

But by then it was too late — the monster had caught him. Taking a deep breath, the monster swallowed the poor puppet as if he were sucking up a raw egg, and he swallowed him with such violence and avidity that Pinocchio was knocked cruelly about inside the Shark's body, leaving him still in a daze a quarter of an hour later.

When he came back to his senses after that shock, he didn't have the faintest idea where he was. All around him was a great darkness — a darkness so black and profound that he felt he had fallen headfirst into a brimming inkwell.

He sat there listening but didn't hear a sound. Every now and then rough gusts of wind whipped across his face. At first he didn't understand where that wind was coming from, but then he realized it came from the monster's lungs. The Shark, you see, suffered terribly from asthma, and when he breathed, it sounded just like the north wind blowing.

Pinocchio at first tried to act brave. But when he confirmed that he was, beyond a shadow of a doubt, trapped in the belly of a sea monster, he began to weep and wail, and through his tears he said, "Help! Help! Oh, poor me! Isn't anyone coming to rescue me?"

"Who do you expect to rescue you, wretch?" said a cracked old voice in the darkness, sounding like an out-of-tune guitar.

"Who said that?" asked Pinocchio, frozen with fear.

"I did! I'm a poor tuna, swallowed along with you by the Shark. And you — what kind of fish are you?"

"I have nothing to do with fish. I'm a puppet."

"Well, if you're not a fish, why did you let yourself get swallowed by the monster?"

"I didn't let myself get swallowed – he just came and swallowed me! And now what are we supposed to do here in the dark?"

"Accept our fate and wait for the Shark to digest us both!"

"But I don't want to be digested!" howled Pinocchio, starting to cry again.

"Neither do I," replied the Tuna, "but I'm rather philosophical, and I take comfort in the thought that, when you're born a Tuna, it's nobler to die in water than in oil!"

"Nonsense!" shouted Pinocchio.

"That's my opinion," replied the Tuna, "and all opinions, as the tuna politicians say, deserve to be respected!"

"No matter what, I want to get out of here. I want to escape."

"Escape then, if you can!"

"This Shark that swallowed us, is he very big?" asked the puppet.

"He's more than a kilometre long – just imagine! – and that's not counting his tail."

As they were discussing these matters in the dark, Pinocchio thought he saw, far off in the distance, a faint glow.

"What in the world could that little light be, way off in the distance?" Pinocchio wondered aloud.

"It must be some companion in misfortune, waiting like us to be digested!"

"I want to go and see. What if it turns out to be some old fish who can show me the way out?"

"I hope with all my heart that you're right, dear puppet."

"Goodbye, Tuna."

"Goodbye, puppet, and good luck."

"Where will we see each other again?"

"Who knows? Some things we shouldn't even think about!"

Chapter 35

As soon as Pinocchio said goodbye to his good friend Tuna, he began fumbling his way on tiptoes through the darkness of the Shark's belly, putting one foot in front of the other, heading for the faint light he could see glowing far in the distance.

As he walked he could feel his feet sinking into puddles of slick, greasy water, which smelled so strongly of fried fish that it reminded him of the middle of Lent.

And the farther he went, the brighter and more distinct the glow became. He walked and walked until at last he reached it – and when he reached it, do you know what he found? I'll give you a thousand guesses. He found a small dining table, on top of which stood a green glass bottle with a burning candle in its neck, and beside which sat a little old man, who looked so white he might have been made of snow, or whipped cream. The man was champing absent-mindedly on some live minnows – so live they occasionally jumped right out of his mouth as he chewed.

This sight filled poor Pinocchio with such great and unexpected happiness that he was just a whit away from becoming delirious. He wanted to laugh, he wanted to cry, he wanted to say a mountain of things. But instead he whimpered confusedly and stammered out a few broken and incoherent words. Finally he managed to let loose a shout of joy, and, opening his arms wide and flinging them around the little old man's neck, he began to yell, "Oh, my dear daddy! I've finally found you again! From now on I won't ever leave you again, not ever, not ever!"

"So my eyes are not deceiving me?" replied the little old man, rubbing his eyes. "So you really are my dear Pinocchio?"

"Yes, yes, it's me, really me! And you've already forgiven me, haven't you? Oh, my dear daddy, how good you are! And to think that I, on the other hand . . . Oh! But if you only knew what misfortunes have rained down on my head and how many things have gone wrong for me! The truth is, poor Daddy, that the day you sold your coat to buy me a spelling book so I could go to school, I ran off to see the puppet show, and the puppet master wanted to throw me on the fire to help roast his ram, and he was the one who ended up giving me five gold coins to bring to you, but I ran into the Fox and the Cat, who took me to the Red Crayfish Inn, where they ate like wolves, and when I left alone

that night I ran into murderers who started chasing after me, and I ran and they chased, and I kept running and they kept chasing, until they hung me from a branch of the Great Oak, where the Beautiful Girl with Sky-Blue Hair sent a little carriage to fetch me, and when the doctors visited they said at once, 'If he's not dead, it's a sign he's still alive,' and then a lie slipped out of my mouth and my nose started growing and wouldn't fit through the door, which is why I went with the Fox and the Cat to bury the four gold coins, one of which I had spent at the inn, and the Parrot started laughing, and instead of two thousand coins I found none, causing the judge when he heard I'd been robbed to send me straight to jail, to reward the thieves, and as I was leaving I saw a nice bunch of grapes in a field, but I got caught in a trap and the farmer, who goodness knows had the right, put a dog collar on me so I could guard his henhouse, then recognized my innocence and let me go, and the Serpent, with the smoking tail, started laughing and burst a vein in his heart, and that's how I went back to the house of the Beautiful Girl, who was dead, and the Pigeon saw me crying and said, 'I saw your daddy building a boat to go and look for you,' and I said, 'Oh, if only I had wings, too!' and he said, 'Do you want to go and see your daddy,' and I said, 'If only – but who will take me,' and he said, 'I'll take you,' and I said, 'How?,' and he said, 'Climb on my back,' and so we flew all night, then in the morning all the fishermen looking out to sea told me, 'There's a poor fellow in a little boat who's about to drown,' and I recognized you right away even from that distance, because my heart told me, and waved to you to come back to shore—"

"I recognized you, too," said Geppetto, "and I would gladly have come back to shore, but how? The sea was rough and a big wave flipped my boat over. Then when the terrible Shark saw me nearby in the water, he raced towards me, snatched me right up with his tongue, and gulped me down like a ravioli."

"And how long have you been trapped in here?" asked Pinocchio.

"From that day on – it must be two years now. Two years, my dear Pinocchio, that seem like two centuries!"

"And how have you managed to get by? And where did you find the candle? And the matches for it – who gave them to you?"

"I'll tell you the whole story. You see, that same storm that flipped my boat over also sank a merchant ship. The sailors were all rescued, but the ship went to the bottom, and this same Shark, who had an excellent appetite that day, after swallowing me, swallowed that ship, too."

"What? Swallowed it whole?" asked Pinocchio, amazed.

"In a single gulp. And the only thing he spit back out was the mainmast, which got stuck in his teeth like a fishbone. Luckily for me, that ship was supplied not only with tins of preserved meat but also hardtack, which is ship bread, bottles of wine, raisins, cheese, coffee, sugar, tallow candles, and boxes of wax matches. Thanks to these gifts from heaven, I've been able to get by for two years. But now I'm down to the last crumbs – the pantry's empty and this candle that you see burning is the last one I have."

"And then?"

"And then, my dear, we'll both be left in the dark."

"In that case, dear Daddy," said Pinocchio, "there's no time to lose. We must quickly think how to escape."

"Escape? How?"

"We'll escape through the Shark's mouth and swim away across the sea."

"That sounds great, my dear Pinocchio, except that I don't know how to swim."

"So? You can climb onto my back, and I'm such a good swimmer that I'll bring you safe and sound back to shore."

"You're dreaming, my boy!" replied Geppetto, shaking his head and smiling sadly. "Do you really think a puppet like you, barely a metre tall, could possibly be strong enough to swim with me on your back?"

"Try it and you'll see! Anyway, if it's written in the stars that we're going to die, at least we'll have the consolation of dying in each other's arms."

And without another word, Pinocchio took the candle, and as he went ahead to light the way, he said to his daddy, "Follow me, and don't be scared."

And so they trekked from one end of the Shark's belly to the other. But when they came to the point where the monster's roomy throat began, they thought it wise to stop and look around and wait for the right moment to escape.

You see, since the Shark was quite old and suffered from asthma and heart palpitations, he had to sleep with his mouth open. So when Pinocchio stood on the edge of the Shark's throat and looked up, he could see, through that enormous gaping mouth, a nice chunk of starry sky and some lovely moonlight.

"This is the right moment to escape," he whispered, turning to his daddy. "The Shark is sleeping like a log, the sea is calm, and it's almost as light as day. So come on, Daddy, follow me and soon we'll be saved."

Wasting no time, they climbed up the sea monster's throat, and once they reached his vast mouth, they began to tiptoe across his tongue – a tongue so wide and so long that it looked like a garden path. They were about to hurl themselves into the sea with a great leap, but just at that very moment the Shark sneezed, and sneezed so violently that Pinocchio and Geppetto were knocked backwards and flung once more to the bottom of the monster's belly.

When they landed with a crash, their candle went out and father and son were left in the dark.

"Now what?" asked Pinocchio, looking serious.

"Now, my boy, we're done for."

"Why? Give me your hand, Daddy, and be careful not to slip!"

"Where are you taking me?"

"We have to try again. Come with me and don't be scared."

And so Pinocchio took his daddy by the hand, and they tiptoed again up to the monster's throat. From there they walked the entire length of his tongue and clambered over the three rows of teeth. Before making the big leap, the puppet said to his daddy, "Climb onto my back and hold on as tight as you can. I'll take care of the rest."

As soon as Geppetto had a firm grip on his son's back, good Pinocchio leapt into the water and began swimming, full of confidence. The sea was smooth as oil. The moon was shining in all its brilliance, and the Shark went on sleeping – a slumber so deep that not even a cannon could have woken him.

Chapter 36

As Pinocchio swam swiftly towards the beach, he realized that his daddy, who was clinging to his back with his legs in the water, was trembling uncontrollably, as if the poor man were suffering from malarial fever.

Was he trembling from cold or from fear? Who can say? Perhaps a little of both. But Pinocchio, thinking he was trembling from fear, tried to comfort him by saying, "Don't worry, Daddy! In a few minutes we'll reach shore and be safe."

"But where is this blessed shore?" asked the little old man, growing more and more anxious, squinting like a tailor threading a needle. "Here I am looking in every direction and I can't see anything but sky and sea."

"But I can see the shore, as well," said the puppet. "For your information, I'm like a cat – I can see better by night than by day."

But poor Pinocchio was only pretending to be in good spirits – in fact he was losing hope. He was running out of strength and breath. He couldn't go on much longer, and the shore was still far away.

He swam until he had no breath left, then he turned his head towards Geppetto and stammered out these words: "Oh, Daddy, help me – I'm dying!"

Both father and son were by now on the verge of drowning, when they heard a voice that sounded like an out-of-tune guitar: "Who's dying?"

"I am – and my poor daddy!"

"I recognize that voice! You're Pinocchio!"

"That's right – and you?"

"I'm the Tuna, your cell mate from the Shark's belly."

"How did you manage to escape?"

"I followed your example. You showed me the way, and I escaped after you did."

"My dear Tuna, you've arrived in the nick of time! I beg you, for the love you bear your little tuna children: help us, or we're done for."

"Gladly, with all my heart. Grab hold of my tail, both of you, and let me pull you. We'll reach the shore in just a few minutes."

Geppetto and Pinocchio, as you might imagine, accepted this invitation at once.

But instead of holding on to his tail, they decided it would be more comfortable to climb right onto his back.

"Are we too heavy?" Pinocchio asked.

"Heavy? Not in the least. I feel like I have a couple of conch shells on my back," replied the Tuna, who was as big and strong as a young bull.

When they reached shore, Pinocchio jumped off first so he could help his daddy get down. Then he turned to the Tuna, and in a voice full of emotion he said, "My friend, you saved my daddy! No words of mine can ever thank you enough! But at least let me give you a kiss, as a sign of my eternal gratitude!"

The Tuna lifted his snout out of the water and Pinocchio, kneeling on the ground, gave him a heartfelt kiss right on the mouth. The poor Tuna, not used to such spontaneous and genuine displays of affection, was so moved that he started crying like a baby, and embarrassed to be seen in such a state, he plunged his head back under the water and vanished.

By this time the sun was up.

As he offered his arm to Geppetto, who was so tired he could barely stand, Pinocchio said, "Just lean on my arm, dear Daddy, and let's be on our way. We'll walk ever so slowly, like ants, and when we get tired we'll rest awhile beside the road."

"And where are we supposed to go?" asked Geppetto.

"We'll look for a house or a hut, where someone might give us, out of charity, a mouthful of bread and a little straw for our bed."

After no more than a hundred paces they saw, sitting by the roadside, two ugly mugs begging for handouts.

It was the Cat and the Fox. But they had changed so much that they were scarcely recognizable. The Cat, you see, had pretended for so long to be blind that eventually he really did go blind. And the Fox was now old, mangy, and completely paralysed on one side – he had even lost his tail. That's how it goes. That wicked thief, after falling on very hard times indeed, found himself one fine day forced to sell his beautiful tail to a travelling salesman, who bought it because he needed a fly-swatter.

"Oh, Pinocchio," shouted the Fox in a whiny voice, "have a little pity on these two poor invalids."

"Invalids!" repeated the Cat.

"So long, charlatans!" replied the puppet. "You fooled me once, but I'll never fall for your tricks again!"

"But it's true, Pinocchio, now we really are poor and wretched!"

"Wretched!" repeated the Cat.

"If you're poor, you deserve it. Remember the proverb that says: *Stolen money never bears fruit.* Goodbye, charlatans!"

"Have mercy on us!"

"... on us!"

"Goodbye, charlatans! Remember the proverb that says: *The devil's flour turns out to be chaff.*"

"Don't leave us alone!"

"... lone!" repeated the Cat.

"Goodbye, charlatans! Remember the proverb that says: *He who steals his neighbour's cloak will die without a shirt.*"

With these words, Pinocchio and Geppetto resumed their calm walk down the road, until, after another hundred paces or so, they saw, at the end of a path, in the middle of the fields, a nice hut made entirely of straw, but with a roof covered with terracotta tiles.

"Someone must live in that hut," Pinocchio said. "Let's go and knock."

They went, and they knocked at the door.

"Who is it?" said a little voice inside.

"We're a poor father and a poor son, with nothing to eat and no place to stay," replied the puppet.

"Turn the key and the door will open," said the little voice.

Pinocchio turned the key, and the door opened. Once inside, they looked around but saw no one.

"Hello? Where is the owner of this hut?" Pinocchio asked, surprised.

"I'm up here!"

Father and son quickly looked up at the ceiling, and there, sitting on a beam, they saw the Talking Cricket.

"Oh, my dear little Cricket!" said Pinocchio, in a friendly voice.

"So now you're calling me your 'dear little Cricket' are you? Do you recall trying to drive me out of your house by throwing a wooden mallet at me?"

"You're right, dear Cricket! Now you can drive me out, you can even throw a wooden mallet at me – but have mercy on my poor daddy."

"I'll have mercy on the father and also on the son. But I wanted to remind you of the cruel treatment I received, to show you that in this world, whenever possible, we should treat others kindly, if we wish to be treated with similar kindness in our hour of need."

"You're right, dear Cricket, you're absolutely right, and I'll never forget the lesson you've taught me. But tell me, how did you manage to buy yourself this beautiful hut?"

"This hut was given to me yesterday by a charming goat, whose fleece was the most beautiful sky-blue colour."

"And where did the goat go?" asked Pinocchio, extremely curious.

"I don't know."

"And when will she be back?"

"She won't ever be back. She was extremely distressed when she left yesterday, and she seemed to be bleating these words: 'Poor Pinocchio – now I'll never see him again! The Shark must have devoured him by now!'"

"She really said that? Then it was her! It was her! It was my dear Fairy!" yelled Pinocchio, sobbing and heaving uncontrollably.

After a good cry, he dried his eyes and prepared a nice bed of straw for old Geppetto to lie down on. Then he asked the Talking Cricket, "Tell me, dear Cricket, where can I find a glass of milk for my poor daddy?"

"Three fields away there's a man named Giangio who has a small farm with some cows. Go to him and you'll find the milk you seek."

Pinocchio rushed to the house of the farmer named Giangio. But the farmer said, "How much milk do you want?"

"I want a full glass."

"A glass of milk costs a penny. You can pay me the penny first."

"I don't have even a penny," said Pinocchio, thoroughly embarrassed and dejected.

"That's bad, my puppet," replied the farmer. "If you don't have even a penny, then I don't have even a swallow of milk."

"Oh well!" said Pinocchio, turning to leave.

"Just a moment," said Giangio. "You and I can work out something. Are you willing to turn a donkey wheel?"

"What's a donkey wheel?"

"It's that wooden contraption, which draws up water from the cistern, so I can water my vegetables."

"I'll try."

"All right, then, pull me up a hundred buckets of water, and I'll give you a glass of milk in exchange."

"OK"

Giangio led the puppet to the garden and showed him how to turn the wheel. Pinocchio went to work at once. By the time he had finished pulling up the hundred buckets he was dripping with sweat from head to toe. Never in his life had he worked so hard.

"Up to now," said the farmer, "this work was done by my donkey, but that poor creature has come to the end of his days."

"Will you take me to see him?" Pinocchio asked.

"Gladly."

As soon as Pinocchio entered the stall, he saw a donkey stretched out on the straw, worn out from hunger and overwork. When Pinocchio had given him a long, hard look, he said to himself, uneasily, "But I know this donkey! I've seen that face before!"

And leaning down towards the donkey, Pinocchio asked him, in asinine dialect, "Who are you?"

Hearing this question, the donkey opened his dying eyes and answered in the same dialect, "I'm La-amp-wi-ick."

Then he closed his eyes and passed away.

"Oh, poor Lampwick!" said Pinocchio softly, and picking up a handful of straw, he wiped away a tear that was rolling down his cheek.

"You're so worked up about a donkey that didn't cost you a penny?" said the farmer. "How should I feel, after paying good money for him?"

"I can explain: he was a friend of mine."

"A friend?"

"A classmate of mine!"

"What?" shouted Giangio, bursting into laughter. "What? You had jackasses for classmates? I can imagine what a fine education you got!"

The puppet, mortified by these words, did not reply. He took his glass of warm milk and went back to the Cricket's hut.

From that day on, for the next five months, he continued getting up every morning, before dawn, so that he could turn the donkey wheel and earn that glass of milk, which was doing so much to improve his daddy's poor health. Nor was this all he did: in his spare time, he learned to weave baskets out of reeds, and by carefully managing the money he made from selling the baskets he was able to cover their daily expenses. On top of that, he built an elegant wheelchair all by himself so that he could take his daddy out for strolls and fresh air when the weather was nice.

And in the evenings, he practised reading and writing. In a nearby village, he had paid a few pennies for a big book, which was missing its title page and index, and that's how he practised his reading. As for writing, he used a sharpened twig for a pen, and lacking both inkwell and ink, he dipped the twig into a little bottle full of blackberry and cherry juice.

Indeed, because of his resolve to do his best and to work hard to get ahead, he not only succeeded in making his daddy's life comfortable but he also managed to save up forty pennies to buy himself a new outfit.

One morning he said to his father, "I'm going to the nearby market, to buy myself a jacket, a cap, and a pair of shoes. When I come home," he added with a laugh, "I'll be so well dressed that you'll mistake me for a rich gentleman."

After leaving the house, he began running happily. Suddenly, he heard someone call his name, and when he turned he saw a pretty snail peeking out from the hedge.

"Don't you recognize me?" asked the Snail.

"You do look familiar."

"Don't you remember the Snail who worked as a maid for the Fairy with Sky-Blue Hair? Don't you recall that night when I came downstairs to give you some light and found you with your foot stuck in the front door?"

"I recall everything," shouted Pinocchio. "Tell me at once, pretty Snail: where did you last see my good Fairy? What is she doing? Has she forgiven me? Does she still remember me? Does she still love me? Is she very far away? Could I go see her?"

To all these questions, asked in a rush and without pausing for breath, the Snail replied with her usual cool, "My dear Pinocchio! The poor Fairy is bedridden in a poorhouse!"

"A poorhouse?"

"Unfortunately. Having suffered a thousand hardships, she is gravely ill and can no longer afford to buy herself even a crust of bread."

"Really? Oh! Such grief you have brought me! Oh, poor Fairy! Poor Fairy! If I had a million pounds, I'd run to give it all to her. But I only have forty pennies. Here they are – I was just going to buy myself a new outfit. Take them, Snail, and carry them at once to my good Fairy."

"And your new outfit?"

"What do I care about a new outfit? I'd sell even these rags I'm wearing if it would help her! Go, Snail, and hurry up! And come back here in two days' time – I hope I can give you a little more money then. Up to now I've been working to take care of my daddy; from now on, I'll work five extra hours per day to take care of my mother, too. Goodbye, Snail, and I'll expect you in two days."

The Snail, contrary to her custom, began running like a lizard beneath the fierce August sun.

When Pinocchio returned home, his father asked him, "Where's your new outfit?"

"I couldn't find one that fit me well. Oh well! I'll buy one another time."

That evening, instead of working until ten, Pinocchio worked halfway through the night, and instead of making eight wicker baskets, he made sixteen.

Then he went to bed and slept. And in his sleep he thought he saw the Fairy in a dream. Beautiful and smiling, she gave him a kiss and said, "Bravo, Pinocchio! Because of your good heart, I forgive you every mischievous thing you've ever done. Children who dotingly look after parents who are poor or sick always deserve great praise and great love, even if they can't be considered models of obedience and good behaviour. Be good from now on and you'll be happy."

At this point the dream ended, and Pinocchio woke with wide eyes.

Now imagine his amazement, readers, when upon waking he realized that he was no longer a wooden puppet, but rather a boy like other boys. He looked around, and instead of the usual straw walls of their hut, he saw a lovely little room furnished and decorated with a simplicity that was almost elegant. Jumping out of bed, he found a fine new suit of clothes laid out for him, along with a new cap and a pair of leather boots that made him look pretty as a picture.

As soon as he was dressed, he naturally thrust his hands into his pockets, and there

he found a little ivory coin purse, on which was written these words: *The Fairy with Sky-Blue Hair returns to her dear Pinocchio his forty pennies and thanks him very much for his good heart.* But when he opened the coin purse, instead of forty pennies, he found forty shining gold pieces, all fresh from the mint.

At this point he went to look in the mirror, and he thought he was someone else. No longer did he see the usual reflection of a wooden marionette; instead he saw the sprightly and intelligent image of a handsome boy with brown hair, blue eyes, and an expression so happy you'd have thought it was his birthday.

Amid all these marvels coming one right after the other, Pinocchio no longer knew whether he was awake or just dreaming with his eyes open.

"And my daddy – where is he?" Pinocchio suddenly yelled. Rushing into the next room, he found old Geppetto: healthy and spry and in good spirits, as in times past. Having already resumed his wood-carving trade, he was at work designing a beautiful picture frame, richly adorned with leaves and flowers and the little heads of various animals.

"I'm curious, dear Daddy. How do you explain all this sudden change?" Pinocchio asked, throwing his arms around him and kissing him.

"This sudden change in our house is all thanks to you," said Geppetto.

"Thanks to me?"

"Yes, because when children who were once naughty become nice, their whole families change and become happier."

"And the old wooden Pinocchio – where is he now?"

"Over there," replied Geppetto, pointing to a big puppet that was propped against a chair, its head lolling to one side, its arms dangling and its legs crossed and bent at the knees. From the looks of it, it would take a miracle to make it stand upright.

Pinocchio turned to see it. And after staring at it for a little while, he said to himself, with enormous satisfaction, "How funny I was, when I was a puppet! And how happy I am now that I've become a proper little boy!"

The End

Carlo Collodi was the pen name of Carlo Lorenzini, who was born in Florence in 1826. The son of a cook and a servant, he began his writing career as a journalist before turning to children's stories. He died in 1890, unaware of the international success that his creation *Pinocchio* would eventually enjoy.

Fulvio Testa is one of Italy's most distinguished artists and illustrators and has had many exhibitions in the United States and Europe. In addition to his own prize-winning titles, he has illustrated books by authors such as Anthony Burgess and Gianni Rodari.

Geoffrey Brock is the prize-winning translator of works by Cesare Pavese, Umberto Eco, Roberto Calasso, and others. He teaches creative writing and translation at the University of Arkansas.

Also illustrated by Fulvio Testa

FULVIO TESTA

Aesop's FABLES

Retold by FIONA WATERS

978 1 84939 049 1

'Fulvio Testa's glorious illustrations are full of vivid colours,
perfect for capturing the attention of young readers . . .
Fiona Waters does a great job of keeping everything lucid
and bringing the stories to a modern audience.'

Carousel Magazine